Targeted

Erin McGaw

Contents

Chapter 1

Present Time

"Can I get another glass of water? Oh, and make sure there's lemon in it this time."

The pretentious undertone in her voice was one I'd fast become used to over the last year, working as a waitress at Crimson Oaks. The restaurant was one that drew in the richer residents in town, with a menu priced high and portions so incredibly small that they were considered worthy of five stars.

"Sure," I said politely, ignoring the snickers of the rest of the guests at the table as I grabbed the empty glasses, "I'll get that for you right away."

Making my way through the rows of tables and towards the kitchen, the soft murmur of the dining room was immediately drowned out as I pushed into the back room. The staff was hard at work – perfectly searing the meat, putting together the meals, and cleaning up as they went along. It was a well-orchestrated system back here, and with the chaos out front, I often found myself envying the people who didn't have to deal directly with the customers.

"Please tell me again why you decided not to book off the night of your birthday?" Lucia asked, sidling up to me with an exasperated look on her face as I leaned against the counter, grabbing a cold pitcher of water. She'd worked as a waitress for three years before being promoted to a kitchen manager, and once I'd started, she'd taken me under her wing – showing me the ropes and giving me a source of sanity during my daily shifts.

"It's not that big of a deal," I shrugged. "I didn't have any other plans, plus, I could use the extra tips from tonight if I want to start enrolling in classes come the fall. Every bit helps."

"At least tell me you're going home to relax once you're done," she pressed, her curiosity fading as a softer expression filled her eyes.

Lucia was all too familiar with my situation. Three years ago, on the day I'd turned eighteen, I'd been left to fend for myself when my time in the foster system had expired. I'd been prepared of course, already having found a cheap apartment on the edge of town and having been saving since I'd been allowed to legally hold down a job. From there on out I'd been on my own. I didn't have any family I knew of, and once I'd graduated high school, with no funds to start at university, I'd taken up a full-time job at a retail market. It was only last winter that I'd applied as a waitress here at Crimson Oaks, quickly earning my serving certifications after I'd been offered the position.

I nodded. "There's a movie and a glass of wine waiting for me at home," I mused, leaning across the counter to grab two slices of lemon before dropping them into the water and placing it on a fresh tray. "But I've still got about an hour left of my shift before I can start thinking about that."

"It'll be over before you know it, and then you'll be able to enjoy what's left of your 21st." Pulling a small envelope out from behind the coffee maker, she slid it towards me with a smile on her face. "And in case you thought I forgot... happy birthday Aspen."

The smile on my face softened marginally as I saw my name scrawled across the front. "Thank you," I said appreciatively, tucking it into the front of my apron so I wouldn't leave it behind, "but I really should be getting back out there."

Once she'd wished me a good night, I balanced the drink tray on my hand and headed back out to finish my shift. Now that Lucia had made me think of the relaxing night I had ahead, it was all that was on my mind as I jotted down orders, delivered food, and settled the bills for my designated section. The minutes seemed to fly by, and as the time on my watch began ticking closer to eight, I started giving away my tables to the other staff when new customers arrived.

It was five after eight when I returned to my last table, pocketing the tip they'd left me as I wiped off the surface and grabbed the last of the dirty dishes. When I reached the break room minutes later, I retrieved my bag from the cupboard I'd stored it in, yanking open the zipper to stuff my apron inside before I grabbed my jacket and headed for the back door.

Despite the early hour in the evening, the sun had long since set and the night sky did little to illuminate the sidewalk as I headed for the train station two blocks up. As I pulled my headphones out of my pocket and turned the volume of my music up loud, I drowned out the noise from the streets as the wind nipped at my cheeks. By the time I reached the station, my nose and the tips of my ears were coloured pink, and when the train pulled up, I managed to snag an open seat next to the window.

As the train began to gain speed – the buildings whizzing by – I tucked my underneath my seat and pulled out the envelope Lucia had given me. Opening it up, the edges of my lips tugged upwards at the sight of the card that had an overflow of balloons on the front.

Happy Birthday Aspen!

Make this year the best one yet, because you deserve it more than anyone ~Lucia

It was rare that I got any form of gift, and even though it was just a kind sentiment, I couldn't help but run my hand over the neatly scrawled words. Flipping it closed a moment later, I tucked it back safely inside the envelope and into my bag.

As the train neared the center of town, more passengers boarded and the narrow walkways were soon filled with people unable to find a seat. This didn't last long however, because once we began venturing further towards the edges of the city – where the run-down streets and the poorer neighbourhoods were located, the crowd started to thin out with each drop-off point we passed.

When we reached the very last stop on the track – my stop – there were only a few people left to get off, including me, an elderly couple, and a man that had been seated a few rows behind me. I watched as the elderly couple headed towards the bus connection the small station had, but as I made a turn to head for the stairs and out towards the streets, I could feel a pair of eyes on me.

A knot of dread twisted in my chest as if on instinct.

There were few things that sent me into paranoia, having toughened my skin through my less than fortunate teen years, but I had also developed a sixth sense to recognize danger. It was dark, the streets weren't all that populated, and knowing that I didn't live in the best area – my apartment still three blocks down the road, I threw a precautionary glance over my shoulder as I turned the corner.

It took only three steps before I saw the man from the train follow my path and my heart spiked with fear. It didn't matter how skilled I was at self-defence, because I wasn't disillusioned enough to think I would be able to take down someone who looked to be twice my age and built like a brick wall.

I quickened my pace, hoping that I had a chance at outrunning him, but when I looked over my shoulder again, all I saw was him speeding up as well.

He was tailing me – which meant that going directly home was not an option.

Cutting across the parking lot of a local mini mart, I sprinted down the next side street, thinking that my change in direction would throw him off course. Not risking a glance back, I pulled my dangling headphones off and tucked them into my pocket as I turned another corner and continued the long way home.

I thought I was safe. I thought I was in the clear.

Circling back around to my block however, it was evidently clear that I wasn't.

The man who'd been following me was standing just a few feet in front of me, and the sound of my boots trampling over the snow-covered road was loud enough for him to hear. I froze, my body flooding with fear as his head snapped upwards, his green eyes piercing and his grin slowly growing to put me on edge.

"There you are," he chuckled, taking a few slow steps towards me, "I thought you'd run off."

I quickly made a move to retreat, but my heart sank when I turned on my heel to see that he was no longer alone. There were three more of them now, all similar in size, but two of them looked closer to my age than the others.

I was surrounded with nowhere to go.

"What do you want?" I yelled, the words paining my throat as they fought to be heard over the howling winds.

My confidence faltered however when I was met with nothing but menacing laughs that tore me down, and feeling completely helpless, I couldn't decide whether to scream or attempt to run.

"What do we want?" one of the younger men said, stepping forward to tower over me. He immediately noticed the way that, while the air was cold, it wasn't the reason why I was shaking so persistently in my boots. "Well, Aspen, I believe the answer to that question would be you."

Hearing my name roll off his tongue caused my eyes to widen and sent a chill straight down my spine. Any notions about getting away momentarily ceased as a myriad of thoughts filled my head. How did they know who I was? Who were they? And most importantly – why were they looking for me specifically?

None of these questions made it passed my lips however, as the man who stood in front of me reached forward to grab my arm. I immediately shrugged him off, stumbling a few steps backwards. An amused expression overtook his face – his eyes scanning over my features as though the idea of me fighting back was unfathomable.

"Give it up, there's nowhere for you to run."

While I knew my chances against the men closing in on me were slim, my mind wasn't wired to just stand there and let them win. That's why, as the man's hand circled my wrist once more, I quickly brought my other arm up, clenching my fingers tightly together before my hand connected with his nose. A yelp of pain left his lips, causing the others to close in on me fast, realizing that things were not going as smoothly as they'd hoped. I felt the man's grip grow slack around my wrist, and my mind – now buzzing with adrenaline, was working in overdrive as everything that followed happened so fast.

Spinning out of the man's hold, I threw another punch to his face, this time my knuckles grazing the skin of his jaw and causing his head to swing backwards. Turning around as I heard another man approaching me, I lunged quickly to the left to avoid his attack. His eyes were lit with anger and rage as they met mine, though the moment he took a step towards me, I spun around, lifting my foot to be level with his abdomen to strike a strong blow.

The two remaining men circling me seemed somewhat impressed that I knew how to hold my own in a fight, though as they eyed each other silently, I could practically hear the words that were left unsaid.

'Get her.'

I gulped, trying to ignore my racing heart as I began to step backwards slowly. My actions caused a sickening grin to curl onto one of the men's lips, while the other seemed entirely focused on the task at hand.

It was the overconfident one that threw a fist first, though with a swift dodge and a knee to his stomach, I managed to avoid his hit. The force behind my attack was low, and with quick determination, he swung again, managing to skim the side of my hip before I could get away. Swaying slightly off balance, I found myself in a position that was perfect for the other man to wrap his arms around my neck, and as I struggled to break free, his hold only tightened.

"Stop moving," he said gruffly, and as the will to fight began to dwindle, I felt his warm breath against my ear as he chuckled. I took in a deep breath, getting prepared to scream, but before a sound could leave my mouth, one of his hands covered my airway. "Don't even think about it."

Closing my eyes, I felt powerless. I could feel the hot sting of tears building behind my eyelids as I concluded that this was it – that tonight would end with torture or death, neither of which were how I envisioned my 21st birthday rounding down to.

Without opening my eyes, I could hear the other men begin to pick themselves up and shake themselves off. Know that it was once again four against one, I knew there was no hope.

"The boss will be here in five," one of them said, having clearly notified whoever they were working for that they'd completed their part of the job.

Just as a low chatter began amongst the four of them about what would happen next, they all went silent.

"I don't think she'll still be here when your boss shows up."

The new voice startled me, and when I opened my eyes, I saw two men not that much older than myself standing a few feet away. They were dressed in all black, and while they didn't have the same rough exterior as the men that had previously surrounded me, the gun holster around their waists caused an ounce of dread to pool in my stomach.

As the hold on my neck tightened, the hand that had been previously covering my mouth fell as the man behind me chuckled. "You're cutting it a little close with the rescue here boys. If I didn't know any better, it seems like you wanted us to have the unfair advantage."

Although I knew I had the freedom to scream for help, any call for help became lodged in my throat as the word rescue stood out to me. What was happening, and why did I just so happen to be stuck in the middle of it?

Even from a distance, I noticed the way that one of the men's eyes narrowed and shoulders tensed as a response. "We'll see about that."

As one second ticked to the next, the two suddenly burst into action, running towards us with intensity burning through their veins. Their attacks were calculated and skilled – their punches powerful and their blows forceful, and when only the man that stood behind me was left standing, I was stuck staring at them, my eyes wide with disbelief.

When their attention turned towards me, I held my breath, bracing myself for what was to come. Shock spread through me seconds later, because instead of targeting me, a punch was directed next to my face, successfully hitting the man behind me square in the jaw. As he stumbled backwards, I was thrown to the side, though I managed to keep my balance as I watched the two men attack the older man with repetitive blows to the face and gut.

My heart was beating erratically as I watched the scene unfold in front of me, but when I snapped out of my state of shock, I quickly realized that I was no longer the main point of attention. Taking it slow at first, I backed away one foot at a time, but once I reached a fair distance away from them, I spun on my heel and made a run for it.

My breathing was heavy and the sound of my feet hitting the snowy pavement was what I focused on – one foot after the other as I didn't dare look back.

By the time I reached my apartment, it took me three times to correctly tap in the security code for the front door as my fingers shook with leftover adrenaline before I heard a welcoming buzz and made it safely into the building. Taking the elevator up to the third floor, I quickly clambered inside my apartment, slamming and locking the door behind me.

Releasing a long-winded sigh, I leant back against the wooden door, my knees collapsing beneath me as I sunk to the floor, trying to make sense of everything that had just happened. The mental images of the men were ones that would be hard to wash from my memory, and knowing that they knew who I was terrified me. I was certain I'd never seen any of them before, and I wasn't someone who frequented social media. I kept to myself, and for good reason.

Despite the fact that my brain was still whirling minutes later, I slowly rose to me feet. A wave of uneasiness washed over me, and hoping some part of it could be rectified by curbing my hunger, I made my way to the kitchen to scour over the few options I had on hand. When I opened the fridge however, the bottle of wine I'd bought for tonight was what caught my eye. I reached for it on instinct, knocking the fridge door closed with my hip as I grabbed a glass and poured myself a generous amount.

The first taste alone was enough to begin to calm the madness inside my head, and as I sank down into the sofa, sipping generously from the glass, I tried to push away what had happened to the dark corners of my mind and just relax.

It was a lost cause however, because even as I begun to feel a faint buzz flowing through my veins from the alcohol, my heart was still beating with fear. I could feel the dull pain in my hip from where I'd been hit, and it was almost as if the stranger's arms were still secured around my neck – holding tight and suffocating me. It was overwhelming, and I hadn't noticed that I had completely zoned out until a sharp, heavy knock on my door broke me from my trance.

I sat silently as the knocking continued, the realization of who was on the other side of that door freezing my movements. Those men tonight had known my name, what I looked like, and where my train let off – so who was to say they didn't know where I lived as well?

"I know you're in there Aspen."

The voice was recognizable, and while I knew it belonged to the person who had ended up saving me, I wasn't taking any chances. He still knew who I was, and if that wasn't a red flag, I didn't know what was.

Moving shakily from the couch, I reached for my phone, bringing up the dial pad as my finger hovered over the number 9. "I'm calling the police if you don't leave in the next five seconds."

There was silence for a few moments, and for a brief second I thought that he'd listened, but when a loud crack reverberated through my apartment, a scream escaped my lips as I saw him break through the door.

"I can't let you do that." He was alone now, his partner nowhere to be seen, and while he didn't seem to want to hurt me in anyway, he'd still broken into my apartment. "You need to come with me. It's not safe for you here now that those guys know where you live."

Although I'd seen what he was capable of and wasn't blind to the gun that rested snug against his hip, I couldn't help the snort that escaped me. "You're crazy if you think I'm going anywhere with you."

My fingers began to dial 9-1-1, but just before I could hit the last number, my phone was lifted from my grasp and the man had locked me against his chest in a loose hold. The initial contact caused me to stumble, but when I saw him pull a needle out of his pocket, my eyes widened in alarm.

"What are you doing?"

"Sorry," he said, though I didn't see an ounce of remorse in his eyes as he plunged the needle into the side of my neck, "but it's for your own good."

The words rang clear in my ears, replaying over and over as I felt my eyes falling shut and my limbs going numb. Before I knew it, all I could hear was a dull ringing in my ears as my surroundings faded to black and I lost consciousness.

Chapter 2

A brain-splitting headache overtook my senses as I slow-ly came to. It felt like I was stuck in an in between period – my ears ringing loudly as I stayed surrounded by darkness, and the only thing that seemed to be working was my mind as it clung to a specific memory from my past.

I was remembering the last time I had felt like this. This helpless. This much in pain.

It had happened in the second group home I'd been sent to after my adoptive parents had been killed in a car accident. The caretakers were clever in the sense that they acted as though they were responsible and caring when the social workers visited, but when the doors to the home were locked and no one was there to see, they had no rules. They didn't care for us, barely giving us enough food to survive as they saved the money they were getting all for themselves.

As a child, I'd been quiet, and even after my parents died I kept up that persona, until one night two months into my stay at the group home. I'd been minding my own business, sitting in the back corner of the yard with a book in my lap, trying to appear as small and insignificant as possible to hide from the other kids. It was no use however, as two of the older boys found me that afternoon, and they were looking for some form of sick amusement. They'd grabbed the book I'd been reading – the one that my dad had read to me most nights before bed, and held it tauntingly above my head.

"What'cha gonna do about it?" they had teased, laughing as they believed I would just sit back and take their bullying.

I remembered squeezing my small hands into fists and asking for the book back, but when they'd shrugged me off, I'd had enough. All the pent-up anger and emotions I'd kept inside came out at that moment, as I fought the best I could at that age, which ended up not being much. However, it was enough for the two boys, who were only two years older than me, to understand that I wouldn't cower down to them.

The rest of that day was a blur of fighting and flashing lights, and when all was said and done, I'd ended up in the hospital with my first concussion, a broken wrist, and a disappointed social worker telling me that I was being transferred to yet another home.

When I opened my eyes this time though, I wasn't an eight-year old girl. I was a twenty-one-year-old woman, and though there was a faint smell of antiseptic wafting through the air, I knew that I couldn't possibly be in a hospital. Blinking slowly, the mint colouring of the walls was quick to throw my mind for a loop, knowing that the walls of my apartment were all the same stark shade of white.

It was only when the rest of the room came into focus – the other beds lined up beside mine, the large pane glass windows that covered the entire opposite wall, and the looming wooden door at the right side of the room, that everything came rushing back.

The men on the street. The fight. The man coming to my apartment.

Drawing in a sharp breath, I sat up with a fright. My eyes frantically moved around the room, looking for some sort of sign as to where the hell I was. My heart beat sped up as I realized I was all alone, and though I figured I mustn't be the only person in the entire building, from the vast amount of forest that was visible through the windows, I knew I wasn't anywhere close to my apartment.

Just as I was about to throw my legs out from underneath the blanket that had bunched up around my waist, the large doors creaked open. My movements froze as a girl, seemingly my age, walked into the room with a tray in her hands. My focus was on her as she continued moving towards me, and it was only when she looked up and her eyes met mine that she realized I was awake.

Her steps slowed and her eyes widened. "You're awake," she stated, a sense of relief in her voice as a small smile pulled at her lips. The seconds ticked by as I let her words hang in the air, but even with thousands of questions spinning around in my head, I found myself doing nothing but clenching my fists into the blankets. A mixture of concern and confusion flooded her vision as she placed the tray in her hands on the table next to my bed and turned towards me, her forehead creased. "Are you okay?"

Breathing in deeply, I began to nod slowly. "I think so," I trailed, my voice just above a whisper, but with the way my leg began to shake, I knew my words couldn't be farther from the truth.

The last thing I remembered was being attacked, getting away, and then dropping unconscious in the arms of a stranger in my apartment. I wasn't okay – not even close.

It was as if the girl sensed this, her eyes scanning my features intently before she took a step back to give me space. She leant up against the edge of the bed next to mine, letting the silence drag on for a while more before asking in a serious tone, "What do you remember?"

"Everything," I replied, my voice quivering. I didn't sound like myself – all worried and reserved. It'd been a long time since I cowered away from a situation, but this, whatever it was, was something I just couldn't wrap my head around. "I got off the train and was followed by this guy, and I guess a few others since they were all waiting for me. I tried to fight, and when two others showed up I thought I was safe. I got home, locked my doors, but it wasn't enough. Someone came by my apartment, broke down my door, and the last thing I remember was calling 9-1-1 before completely blacking out."

The longer I spoke, the angrier I got. Not only had my birthday been completely ruined by a fluke attempt at kidnapping, but someone had disrespected my privacy, broken into my house, and somehow knocked me out cold and dragged me away to god knows where.

It was only then that I realized that this girl, whoever she was, probably already knew all of this. My eyes snapped upwards, and my suspicions were confirmed as I saw not even a flicker of surprise pass over her features.

Before I could ask anything more, another voice overpowered my own. "Kira?"

My gaze flitted towards the doorway, and though a chill ran down my spine at the sight of him, I couldn't stop the fury from spreading through my veins.

"You."

It was him alright. The young man who'd helped me escape the exchange on the streets and had followed me back to my apartment. He was the reason I was here right now and not in the comfort of my own place.

Although it was clear that he'd been looking for the girl next to me, when he noticed I was awake his steps halted, seemingly unbothered as his eyes pierced into mine. Without giving it a second thought, I sprung from my position on the bed and marched towards him.

"What did you do?" I exclaimed, anger dripping from each word as I got closer. My hands clenched into fists, and when he didn't immediately answer, any sense of control I had left snapped. I raised my arm, bringing it back before pushing my fist forward with the target of his face.

Just as my knuckles grazed his chin however, I felt a pair of arms circle my waist and pull me backwards, causing the tail end of my punch to hit nothing but air.

"Let me go," I said, twisting aggressively until I pulled myself from the girl's hold, whose name I took to be Kira.

"It's okay," she said levelly.

"Okay?" I repeated incredulously. "He – "

"I know," she continued firmly, cutting me off before turning her gaze to the right. "I don't really think now is the best time Beckett."

His gaze flitted to me momentarily and while his expression stayed blank, there was a vague humour that danced across his pupils as I narrowed my eyes and crossed my arms in defense. "I can see that," he replied, his voice low and strong. "When you're done here, you know where to find me."

Nothing else was said as he turned and headed back out the door. Turning towards Kira, I lifted an eyebrow questioningly. She sighed. "I was going to explain."

"Were you?"

"Yes," she replied with no hesitation, "but please tell me that you're not going to freak out."

"Not if you just tell me what's going on," I exhaled, dragging a hand through my hair.

Heading back over to the bed I'd been allotted, I grabbed the bottle of water that had been on the tray that Kira had brought in, taking a swig as she began to explain. "I don't know a whole lot about why those men are after you, but I do know that for the last six months we've had agents tailing you to make sure that you weren't attacked."

"Wait," I cut her off, shaking my head with wide eyes, "after me?"

Kira nodded. "That attack wasn't random." I let out a shaky breath at this information. "We got word of it a few months back, and ever since then we've been on the lookout. There's been attempts in the past, but the agents responsible for watching over you have always gotten to them first."

"Agents?"

"Central intelligence agents belonging to Division 27 under the Strategic International Covert Operations, better known as S.I.C.O."

I snorted. "Unfortunate name."

Kira's lips tilted upwards slightly. "We've heard that before," she said, the amusement of the acronym not lost on her. "This organization isn't well-known. What the people on the streets know is that CIA and MI6 agents are responsible for government run covert operations, but we're a better kept secret."

The CIA? That would mean... "So, what? You guys are spies?"

"That's one name for us. There are people who focus on gathering intel on other organizations and criminals, there are those who are put right in the line of duty – the ones that go out and protect people on a day-to-day basis, there are people who go undercover for years to help make the world a better place, and then there's people like me, who prefer to stay here and work with the research that the organization works hard to keep under wraps."

As Kira's words registered in my head, my initial instinct was to believe that she was lying. None of what she was saying could be true. It couldn't be. But as things began to connect – small things, like how the two agents had shown up to help me that night and how they hadn't actively been trying to hurt me, I started to believe her.

"Okay," I started, and even though I couldn't even begin to process and accept what she was saying, I kept my voice steady. "Let's say you're telling the truth, what does any of this have to do with me?"

"I'm sorry, I don't actually know all that much about why those agents were assigned to protect you other that what I told you. As far as I know, you just showed up on our radar and haven't left."

That wasn't the response I'd been hoping for. I was looking for answers, but looking at the girl across from me, her auburn hair brought together in a tight ponytail and a look of sincerity in her eyes, I knew I wouldn't find them with her.

"What I can tell you though," she continued, "is that even though you may not think so, this is that safest place for you right now."

"Where even is here?"

Sliding off the bed, I padded across the floor towards the windows. There wasn't much that gave a hint as to where we were, though from the old stone that built up the vast towers and the expanse of forest that surrounded the building, I figured this place was well hidden, and had been for years.

"That's something I can't exactly tell you yet," Kira responded, and I glanced over my shoulder to see her looking at me with a hint of sympathy. "But, if you want, after the nurse has checked you over, I can show you around the grounds a bit."

A nod was all it took for me to respond, and as she left me to myself, I let my gaze veer back towards the window. Outside, I could see a few teenagers wandering near the forest line, as well as two middle-aged men walking along one of the footpaths, dressed in black with their heads close together to keep their conversation private. It was like I was being thrown into another world. One that didn't make sense and one where I didn't belong.

Mentally, emotionally, and physically exhausted, I wandered back towards the bed I'd woken up in. There was no way that I'd be able to sleep with my brain currently working in overdrive to process everything that had happened, but that didn't stop me from settling into my blankets and resting my head against the pillow in hopes that a bit of rest would help me think clearer.

"And this is the Grand Hall," Kira said as the two of us walked into what seemed to be nothing more than an upscale cafeteria.

When the nurse had come to check on me, I'd been a restless mess. Trying to relax hadn't done much for me, and since I hadn't wanted to get lost in the building that appeared to be as big as a castle, I'd stayed put. I'd paced up and down the length of the room more times than I could count, muttering under my breath as I attempted to set my thoughts straight. The nurse had immediately sat me down and got my breathing to even out before going over my vitals to make sure that nothing was seriously wrong. Kira had shown up just minutes later, and once I'd been given the okay to leave, I followed behind her down a large set of stones steps.

After being shown where a few of the classrooms and general research labs were located, as they were the closest to the infirmary, our next stop had been the Grand Hall.

It was relatively busy as groups of people gathered around the food counters before finding an empty place to sit. What struck me as surprising however, was the fact that it wasn't just teenagers and young adults taking up the space, but people of all ages, all dressed almost the exact same in mostly black clothing. Still wearing the same white long sleeve that I'd worn for my shift at Crimson Oaks, I stood out, and judging from the curious looks that people gave me as I hovered next to Kira in the entryway, I was certainly gaining some form of attention.

"Are you hungry?" Kira asked, turning to me with a raised eyebrow.

Although I hadn't eaten in who knows how long, food was the last thing from my mind in that moment.

I'd calmed down slightly, but that by no means meant that what Kira had told me just hours before had left my mind. I was in a building meant for people specializing in covert operations, and that fact alone left an unsettling feel in my stomach.

"No," I said, forcing out my reply with as much conviction as I could, "I'm good for now."

Kira's eyes focused on me for a moment, and while I'm sure she could tell that I was lying, she let the subject drop as she led me out of the Grand Hall.

For a while, as she continued to point out different facilities and rooms that we passed, it felt as if I was simply touring a university campus with a guide. She'd pointed out a common room, a high-tech computer lab, as well as where the living quarters were located. That mindset was quickly broken however, when we poked our heads into a lesson and I saw the different forms of interrogation scrawled across the blackboard.

This wasn't a university – not even close.

"How large is this place?" I asked in awe as we strolled along one of the footpaths outside the building. The building had four wings to it – each with its own looming tower, and that didn't even include the smaller barn-like structures that seemed to be scattered over the grounds.

A light chuckle left Kira's lips. "It's overwhelming at first," she started, "but everyone lives on the grounds, so the place has to be big enough for housing, to accommodate schooling for the younger recruits, and then all of our labs, practice facilities, and offices. Our Division owns most of the land surrounding the building, running far into the forests, and it's a necessity considering what some of the people here do on a daily basis. We need all the privacy and space we can get."

I nodded with a vague understanding, and before I could ask anything more, a girl no more than sixteen stopped us in our path. Her eyes flickered to me with a vague interest and curiosity, but after a fleeting moment, she turned to Kira and began to talk. My eyes widened as the words that spilled from her mouth were fluent in another language – possibly German or Russian, I couldn't be sure. What really threw me for a loop was when Kira answered easily in the same language, leaving me speechless as the girl nodded, spinning sharply on her heel as she let us be.

It wasn't lost on me that we were suddenly backtracking as Kira led me towards one of the barns situated near the far end of the grounds, right next to the forest line, but I didn't mention it as I asked, "So, how many languages do you know?"

A small smirk pulled at her lips. "Seven, fluently, and then I'm trying to pick up Chinese and Japanese," she replied, laughing as she noticed my eyebrows raise high with surprise. "You'll figure out pretty quickly that most people around here are fluent in a few different languages. It just helps us do what we do."

The unsettling feeling that had slowly been diminishing came back with a vengeance at the realization that she was talking as though I would be sticking around. My life hadn't always been the greatest, with only a few high points that I held near to my heart, but this insanity – this world that Kira seemed to live in, it wasn't me.

I stayed silent, walking in stride with Kira until she stopped, her hand reaching forward to gain a hard grip on the sliding metal door in front of us. "This," she began as she forced the door to slide open, "is the training barn."

And although it looked like an old barn on the outside, the inside was nothing if not intense.

There was training equipment set up around the edges – punching bags, weights, and machines galore, and out near the back of the space was a complex array of bars, nets, and barriers set up to look like training courses. These areas were taken up by younger people, practicing their skills and gaining their strength, but the center of the room was where my gaze was drawn.

There were numerous men and women matched together as they fought, either hand to hand combat or with sparring sticks in their disposal. The agility and strength these people had was astounding as I noticed a calculation and swiftness behind every move made, but as my eyes roamed from pair to pair, they were always pulled back to two men near the back of the crowd. It was evident that one fighter had a clear upper hand – a blatant aggressiveness behind each step he made that put him on top. He kept his fists close to his chest, blocking his opponent's advances instead of making his own, but in the split second that his opponent left himself vulnerable, he attacked. He lowered his body, spun on his heel and lifted his left foot in an impressive aerial kick that landed right on the jaw of his opponent, knocking him to his knees.

He didn't stop there though. He leaped to his feet, regaining his position to strike again, and only held back as his opponent bailed out.

"Taking an interest in fighting?" Kira mused, knocking my focus off the pair and back to her.

"It's just so..."

"Intense?" she finished for me, to which I nodded in response. "It's like that because if they can't master their technique in here, they know that they won't stand a chance out there."

As the training continued, Kira led me further into it. "So, what are we doing here?"

"Well," she begun, glancing back over her shoulder as I trailed behind her, "I've got to be somewhere for a while, so I thought I'd hand you off to someone you already seem to have gotten acquainted with."

My brows furrowed. "What do you mean?"

There was no need for her to answer though, because while I was confused, everything fell into place as Kira stopped in her tracks. She'd led me over to the pair of fighters that I'd been watching, and while I hadn't had the best view of them when we'd been hovering near the doors, that wasn't a problem now.

The man who'd won was now unwrapping the tape that he'd secured on his hands, but as Kira called out his name and gained his attention, I gritted my teeth in annoyance as the anger I felt about being stuck in this situation resurfaced.

It was Beckett.

Chapter 3

"Beckett."

His gaze was sharp as he turned towards us, looking as though he was still in fighting mode. Realizing it was just us, I noticed his shoulders relax slightly, but his expression remained blank and unconcerned. "What?"

"I've got to meet Collins in the lab in a few minutes, so I need you to watch Aspen."

"Why me?" he asked in an unimpressed tone at the same time that I said, "No way."

Our gazes snapped towards one another, though while his eyes narrowed and flashed with aggravation, I simply crossed my arms and stood my ground defensively.

Undeterred by both of our protests, Kira turned to me with a stern expression. "I'm sorry, but I'm not leaving you alone," she said firmly, leaving no room for an objection before her words were directed towards Beckett. "And as for you, you've been on her security detail for months, so this won't be much different," she explained. "Plus, I don't think Catherine would be very pleased if she heard you let her wander the grounds on her own."

Kira's features were challenging as she waited for a response from Beckett, though from her confidence, she knew he wouldn't refuse. I didn't know who this Catherine was, but whoever she was, she clearly meant something to Beckett, because while I noticed a vein in his neck tick with irritation, he also nodded stiffly after a few moments.

"Fine," he said gruffly.

A smug smile grew on Kira's lips. "Great," she chirped, and with a pointed look in my direction, she let the air around us thicken with tension as she turned to walk away.

"Don't I get a say in this?" I asked loudly and with disbelief.

"Sorry, but no," she replied, waving quickly before disappearing through the barn doors.

Trying to push down my irritation, I turned back to Beckett only to see his retreating back moving away from me. For a split second I thought that this could be a chance for me to leave, but even I knew Kira's worries about me wandering around on my own were warranted. This place was huge, and truthfully, I hadn't been paying all that much attention when Kira had walked me through the main passageways.

"Are you coming?" Beckett asked, stopping near the edge of the barn to glance back over his shoulder at me.

Annoyance flared through my veins as I stomped over towards him, but before I could reach him, he started moving again. His strides were purposeful, and when I finally managed to catch up with him, he didn't spare me a second glance.

"You didn't think you could, oh, I don't know, wait for me?" I asked in a huff of anger.

"Pay better attention and you won't fall behind."

So far, I had managed to control my bubbling anger, but in the presence of Beckett, my temper was being tested. That left me with two choices – either let my rage continue to grow until I couldn't control it, or direct my emotions to another priority, like getting answers. Kira didn't do much in terms of explaining why exactly I was here, just what had happened, and though I didn't like the option, I had a strong feeling that Beckett knew much more.

"So..." I trailed once we were back inside, "Any chance of you telling me why you broke into my apartment last night?"

"No," he replied quickly, his voice low. "And it wasn't last night, it was the night before."

"Wait, what?"

His steps slowed as he turned to look at me, only to see that my eyes were wide at this new information. He furrowed his eyebrows slightly. "Didn't the nurse tell you that you were out for about a day and a half?"

"No," I whispered, still in shock, "she didn't."

For a moment, I thought I saw the resemblance of compassion cross Beckett's features as my eyes met his, but it quickly disappeared as his eyes turned dark and his expression mirrored a blank canvas. He didn't say a word, simply continuing down the hallway looking more tense and uncomfortable than he had previously.

The fact that I'd been unconscious longer than I'd believed had me feeling slightly wary, and as I caught up to Beckett once again, I knew I could've continued to push for answers, but I stayed silent.

Unlike the way Kira had pointed out the rooms we passed and how she'd dropped little factoids about Division 27 into our conversation, Beckett did nothing. He simply marched forward with a purpose, checking to make sure I was still following him every now and then, and as the minutes passed, the silence was enough to bring a spark back to the irritation that had begun to fade.

"I thought you were supposed to be showing me around," I commented sarcastically. "Right now, all I'm seeing is a bunch of closed doors and dusty hallways."

"Just because Kira pawned you off on me, that doesn't mean I'm obligated to listen. I have better things to do then become your own personal tour guide."

"What, you mean beating the shit out of people? Didn't really seem like you needed much more practice."

He glanced my way, raising an eyebrow. "Impressed?"

A noncommittal sound rose from the back of my throat. "If you were so busy," I started, ignoring his comment and the way he so easily flipped between sarcastic and serious, "why even listen to Kira in the first place?"

"Because god forbid I left you to fend for yourself. This isn't some place you can just wander around. There's things you can't see, things you probably don't want to see, and things that would probably scar you for life."

I narrowed my eyes. "I wouldn't even be here if it weren't for you."

"Let's get something straight," he started forcefully, "I brought you here for your own good, because whether you like it or not, you're safer here. I didn't do anything other than my job, and if you have a problem with that, bring it up with the Head of the Division."

Just as I was about to point out the fact that I had no idea who that was, my retort was lost on my tongue. Beckett led me around a corner to a tall spiraling staircase built directly into the stone, and while he began to take the steps two at a time, my climb was much more hesitant.

As we reached the top, the hallway widened once again into a small landing that housed multiple offices. All the doors were shut tight, but with a glance at the plaques next to them, it was clear that this was where the influential people of this place resided. Following behind Beckett, my thoughts were confirmed as we stopped at the very last office and I took a moment to read the plaque that hung to the left.

Catherine Sommers. Head of Division 27.

Now I knew who Beckett was worried about disappointing.

With two hard knocks on the door, Beckett didn't wait for a response before turning the doorknob and entering the room.

The conversation came to a halt as two sets of eyes turned towards us – one belonging to a middle-aged man dressed in a similar fashion to Beckett and the other belonging to a woman I assumed to be Catherine. She wore a pair of black pants and a tight black blazer, though the red shirt that peeked out from underneath was both surprising and refreshing. Not a word of complaint left her lips at our interruption, but I found myself unnerved at the fact her gaze latched onto me and never wavered.

The man, on the other hand, let his gaze flicker between Beckett and I for a moment, understanding filling his features before he looked back to Catherine. "We'll talk later," he said, waiting until she nodded to start towards us. "Donovan," he continued as he clapped his hand on Beckett's shoulder, "I think it's best that we leave these two women alone to talk."

While he at least spared me a glance, barely a few seconds passed before Beckett stepped away from me and followed the man out of the room.

I gulped as I watched the door close on the two of them, slowly turning back to face Catherine. She didn't look particularly dangerous, though there was no question to the fact that she held authority, and that alone was intimidating. Her sleek black hair was pulled back into a tight ponytail, her stance was strong and her features were serious, though as my hesitant eyes met hers, I saw an unrecognizable emotion flicker across them.

"Aspen," she said welcomingly, holding out her hand in greeting, "I was starting to wonder when you'd find yourself here."

"It wasn't exactly by choice," I mumbled still loud enough for her to hear as I averted my gaze but still shook her hand.

With a wry tilt of her lips, she took a step back and nodded towards the desk behind her. "I know this place can be a little intimidating, and it's a lot to take in," she begun, rounding the desk and taking a seat as I nervously sat down across from her.

"That's an understatement."

She nodded in agreement. "It may very well be, but that doesn't change the fact that you're out of your element here. Trust me, I was younger than you when I first stepped foot in this building, and it was overwhelming." Silently agreeing, I didn't speak because while she paused, the calculating look that crossed her features told me she was simply trying to figure out how to put her thoughts into words. "I want you to be comfortable here," was what she ended up settling one, "so if you have any questions, I'd be happy to answer them."

There were a lot of ways that I could've responded – a myriad of questions swirling around in my head that had yet to be answered, but one stood out above the rest. "Who were the guys that attacked me?"

A flicker of surprise lit up her eyes at my bluntness, though it quickly morphed into a shadow of anger. "They were part of the Gemini Clan."

"The... who?"

"The Gemini Clan," she repeated. Intent concentration replaced my confusion as I watched her sigh, looking as though this was the last thing she wanted to be talking about. "A long time ago, an underground branch of central intelligence was created to deal with situations that the government wasn't equipped to handle. There were ethical issues that needed to be crossed to get certain jobs done, so a few agents from the CIA and MI6 came together to form the organization for Strategic International Covert Operations."

"S.I.C.O began to flourish, but with everything that was going on, the original founders didn't notice that one of their agents had turned his back on them. He started the Gemini

Clan, and even when he was caught and sentenced to death, it was too late to stop the Clan from expanding." She took a breath, shaking her head solemnly. "The people that S.I.C.O was formed to protect the world from began to turn our own members, and now, even though we don't acknowledge it, they're known as Division 13."

Horror creeped through my veins as my eyes widened. "You mean," I stuttered, "this place is associated with them?"

"Officially no," she replied confidently. "Division 13 was disbanded from S.I.C.O years ago, but looking back in history, yes, we've had traitors who've helped build up the Gemini Clan."

It was a lot to digest as I sat there gripping the arm rests of my chair. It was a few moments later when I mustered up the courage to ask, "so what do they want with me?"

"I'm not sure," she replied, a hard edge to her words. "We've got our sources on how to figure out what the Gemini Clan is up to and what they're next moves are, so when your name begun floating around late last year, I assigned a group of agents to watch out for you."

"And now that I'm here?"

That was the question that had been eating me up inside since the moment I stepped into the office. I wasn't one of them – I couldn't be. Sure, I knew the basics of fighting, and maybe if I tried hard enough I could string together a few sentences in Spanish, but everything else was out of my league.

"It's really your choice Aspen," she explained. "You're welcome to join in on the beginner classes right away or simply look around and gain your footing, but I would advise getting involved in something while you're here to keep your mind off the Gemini Clan."

I honestly didn't think that was possible, because now that I knew a group of psychopaths were after me, it was all I could think about.

What did they want? Why were they so focused on me? How long would this last?

While I desperately wanted the answers, as I lifted my gaze to meet Catherine's, there was a large part of me that knew once the information was out there, there'd be no turning back.

After succumbing to the hunger that was quickly taking over my body, it was a wonder how I managed to find my way to the Grand Hall. This building was a maze, and one that, apparently, I'd have to master quickly.

Catherine had given me directions as I left her office, but I knew that I must've taken a wrong turn somewhere, as I very quickly found myself mindlessly wandering down the halls. Turn after turn I was graced with nothing but empty, dimly lit hallways, but when I eventually found myself in the midst of a small crowd, I took to following them.

The Grand Hall appeared to be just as busy as it had been earlier, and as I made my way towards the food counter closest to me, trying to draw the least amount of attention possible, I could still feel the numerous pairs of eyes burning into my back.

Ignoring the stares, I stopped in front of the salad bar, throwing together a few things in a bowl before filling a plate with pasta and grabbing a bottle of lemonade. Noticing an empty table near the far left corner of the room, I gripped my tray and hoped that, as I sat down, I'd be left well enough alone.

Nobody seemed to want to bother with me, which caused me to breathe a sigh of relief as I dug into my food, however, luck was only on my side for so long. Just as I finished up my salad and took my first forkful of pasta into my mouth, a looming figure cast a shadow across the table.

Flicking my gaze upwards, my mouth went dry as I saw the man standing across from me. He sported a bruised jaw, visible through the stubble on his face, and with the sleeves of ink that ran up and over his muscled arms before disappearing under his tight black t-shirt, he looked dangerous. Somewhere between blond and brown, his messy hair tumbled over his temples while his piercing green eyes caught my attention as they gave me a calculated once over.

"Hey," I said warily, watching his eyebrows draw together.

Awkwardness filled the air between us as he didn't respond, but as I ducked my head to continue eating, his voice cut through the silence. "You're Aspen, right?"

"Um, yeah." I bit my lip nervously. "How do you know that?"

"We don't get many new people around here, so when somebody shows up out of the blue, news gets around quickly," he replied.

"Great," I mumbled under my breath, stabbing at my food with my fork as I realized that everyone probably knew exactly why I was here.

"I'm Finn by the way," he said, throwing his leg over the bench as he took a seat. "So, how are you adjusting to everything?"

The intensity I first noticed started to fade as his features illuminated with genuine curiosity, though at the moment, I didn't need anyone else on my case. "I'm fine," I said sharply.

"Really?" One of his eyebrows rose inquisitively, a spark of amusement in his tone. "Because I remember being completely freaked out when I first learnt that my parents were a part of this craziness."

Tension seeped from my shoulders as I let out a quiet laugh. "Okay, so maybe I'm not completely fine." I dragged a hand through my hair as I sighed. "It's just a lot to take in."

"It can be," he agreed, "especially if you didn't see it coming. A lot of us are here because we have family in the Division, so we were eased into everything, but when there's people like you, you're kind of just thrown in the deep end."

'And expected to swim,' I finished silently. "That sounds about right."

He stood up suddenly, hooking his thumb over his shoulder. "I've got to head out, so I'll leave you alone for now, but if you ever want someone to show you the ropes around here, I'm your guy."

Surprised by his offer since Beckett, who I assumed Finn had a similar role to, wanted next to nothing to do with me, I found my lips turning upwards. "I'll remember that."

Watching as a friendly smile spread across Finn's lips before he turned and headed for the exit, I felt an odd sense of relief wash over me. While a lot of the people I'd met so far seemed to be bound and determined, maybe it was possible that not everyone here was like that.

Chapter 4

Most of my nights were spent in a dreamless state, however, there was one recurring nightmare that had haunted me since the first time I'd spent the night in a group home. It involved two faceless figures walking down an abandoned street at night; one carrying a baby in her arms, and when they reached the end of the road, they simply left the child alone before turning and walking away.

Each time I was an onlooker in the situation and I'd scream for them to come back to their child, but even through the multiple tactics I'd try, they'd just continue to walk away until they vanished in the distance.

It was then that I usually woke up, but this time was different.

Tears of frustration filled my eyes as I glanced back at the small child and the scene began to transform. The child grew and the backdrop flickered to one that I was familiar with, and before long I was watching myself be attacked, completely helpless to do anything about it. I saw the men surrounding me, the terrified look on my face as I tried to fight, and the defeat that made my shoulders sag when I had given up hope.

My chest began to tighten as the vivid memory played out in my dream, and as I saw myself pushed free of my attacker's arms before turning and bolting away from the scene, everything faded to back.

I shot up in bed; my eyes wide open and my breathing heavy. I could feel the cold sweat building up on the back of my neck, and looking around, it didn't help that I was in a room that was virtually unfamiliar to me.

Kira had found me in the Grand Hall about an hour after I had finished eating, because with the warning from Beckett still fresh in my mind, I hadn't taken the chance of wandering around. She'd seemed slightly distracted as she led me towards the housing quarters, and I made sure to make note of which hallways we took as she showed me the private room that had been set up for me.

It hadn't been much – just a bed and a large wooden wardrobe, but after further investigation, I realized that the wardrobe was stocked full of fresh clothes and the room also housed an en-suite bathroom.

Before long, the exhaustion of the day had caught up to me, and despite the early hour in the evening, as soon as my head had hit the pillow I'd been out like a light. Now however, sitting anxiously in the dark, I threw my gaze towards the old-fashioned clock that hung on the wall, making out the two hands pointing upwards.

It was only just past midnight, and there was no way that I was going back to sleep. Not now, and not here.

Slipping out from underneath the covers with a large black sweatshirt hanging loosely from my body, I managed to find some sort of balance and make my way into the bathroom. Clutching at the edges of the sink, I took deep breaths, trying to calm my racing heart as images from my dream continued to haunt my mind, though it didn't seem to do much good.

Turning on the cold water, I cupped my hands under the tap and splashed my face a few times. It was refreshing and startling, but somehow succeeded at quieting the thoughts that were screaming out at me. Risking a glance in the mirror, I appeared frazzled and not myself, noticing a certain intensity gleaming in my eyes that had never been there before.

It was a few minutes later when I walked cautiously back into my room, my arms crossed protectively across my chest as though the atmosphere itself could harm me. But it was too late, because just being here was harming my sanity. The events of the day had settled, and even though everyone had said that this was where I was the safest, I wasn't sure that I believed them.

I was safest in my own apartment, or maybe at Crimson Oaks, where nobody would dare try anything, but certainly not here. Even the name of this organization – S.I.C.O, suggested I'd be crazy to assume otherwise.

Drawn to the large window that gave me a view of the front grounds, I was quick to notice that there was no one wandering around at this time of night. The moonlight alone illuminated the rocky path that led out towards the forest before it begun to narrow and disappear at the treeline, though casting my gaze farther, I saw nothing. Nothing beyond the trees and nothing suggesting there was anything besides this building within the next couple of miles.

Something had to be out there, even if I couldn't see it – a road, a trail, something that would lead me away from this place.

With a sudden burst of determination, I quickly turned on my heel and threw open the door to the wardrobe, pulling out and stepping into the first pair of pants I saw. Grabbing a jacket as an afterthought, I pulled my unruly hair into a loose ponytail, slipped on my shoes, and tiptoed quietly towards my door.

Flipping the lock, I pulled it open carefully, taking extra care to make sure it didn't creak. When it was open just enough for me to peek out into the hall, I looked both ways and trained my ears to hear if anyone was coming, but came up with nothing. Maneuvering myself into the hall, I had both hands flat on the wood as I slowly brought the door to a close, not taking the risk of letting go until I heard the quiet click of the lock.

When one last look confirmed that there was nobody in sight, I began walking left, but even as I stayed light on my feet, a quiet echo could still be heard. The sound of my footsteps bounced off the stones as I made my way towards the front of the building, and when I'd made it as far as the Grand Hall, I breathed a sigh of relief. I knew that I was close, but having not been shown the front courtyard, only the back, this was the furthest I'd gone so far. I'd have to rely on my instincts to guide me the rest of the way.

Figuring heading forwards was the best plan, I only turned when I reached a dead end, and froze when I did so. Picking up on the vague sound of another pair of footsteps, I quickly retreated, pressing my back up against the wall and holding my breath as the steps began to grow louder.

I began to sift through excuses I could use when I was caught – everything from sleep walking to getting lost, but just as the footsteps sounded as if they were right on top of me, they slowly started to quiet down. Slowly releasing the air in my lungs, I took the chance of glancing around the corner, only to notice another hallway that split off just a few feet away from where I stood.

Not willing to test my luck, I waited until I could once again hear silence before continuing on. With only one wrong turn, I eventually found my way to the doors of Division 27 that loomed tall and wide in the entrance hall. Unlocked and heavy, I pushed hard on the antique door handles, ignoring the squeak that filled the air as I stepped out into the night.

Letting the door fall shut with a loud bang, I knew it was only a matter of time before somebody who had heard the noise came investigating, so I took off in a run. There was no time to admire the moon and the stars shining brightly in the sky as I kept to the shadows, following the trail that led towards the forest and hoping the black clothing I wore would be a good enough mask as I crossed the grounds.

By the time I reached the edge of the grounds, I was moving in a full-on sprint – moving my arms back and forth ferociously and pushing my legs to go as fast as they could. I didn't slow down as I snuck between the trees, quickly noting the change of the ground beneath my feet. Instead of smooth grass, I was running atop the unevenness of a forest floor that had tree roots and patches of moss littering it, and rather than risking an injury, I started to slow down to catch my breath.

Leaning back against a tree with my hands on my knees, I looked back to see that the looming building could be seen above the trees. A few lights in the towers were on, and while it was clear that some people called this place home, I wasn't one of them.

Turning my back on Division 27, I marched on.

The night air nipped at my skin as I walked, but thankfully, the further I ventured into the forest, the more the trees helped in shielding the harsher winds as they whistled along above me. Every rustle of leaves or snap of a twig caught my attention, and though my hyperawareness kept me on edge, it also helped in keeping me awake and focused.

It felt like hours had passed when my feet began to ache and I stopped for a moment, taking a seat on top of a large rock. Each way I turned I saw the same expanse of trees, and though I'd been walking a straight line this whole time, it could've been possible that I'd simply been walking in circles.

Shaking that thought from my mind, I waited a while longer before standing up and pushing on forward. I didn't give up, and eventually the light at the end of the tunnel shone as I squinted through the trees and saw some sort of trail that narrowly split the forest ahead.

Finally feeling as though I was getting somewhere, I sped up, following the trail as it grew wider, and when it ended at the edge of an abandoned, winding road, I felt my lips twist upwards.

Success.

Though nothing could be seen except the trees that grew around the road, I certainly felt the increased force of wind, and deciding to walk with the gusts to my back, I headed right. There were no other signs that led me to believe this was the direction I was meant to be moving, but something about it felt right, and I trusted my gut as I walked along the gravel roadside.

The road wound endlessly, but I didn't stray from it, even when the lack of street signs and mile markings struck me as odd. Over time, the weather sent a continuous chill down my spine, and other than pull my thin jacket tighter around me, there wasn't much I could do. I was out here – stranded but determined.

It was less than a minute later when the sound of a rumbling engine hit my ears, causing my muscles to tense up as the headlights lit the road up beside me. The black car with tinted windows slowed to a stop a few feet in front of me, and just as I prepared to put up a fight – believing the driver to be a member of the Gemini Clan, Beckett threw open the driver's door and stepped out.

"Are you insane?"

The fear that had surged through my veins was quickly replaced with anger. He had no right to be here, and there was no way that he was getting his way with me again.

"What are you doing here?" I ground out in return.

"Me?" he asked with disbelief, a dry laugh leaving his lips as he continued. "What are you doing out here, all alone, in the middle of the night?"

Ignoring his question, I threw one back at him. "How did you even find me?"

"Did you really think that just because you'd been brought into the Division that you wouldn't still have people watching out for you? That you wouldn't be seen by security on the thousands of cameras set up throughout the Division?" His questions were thrown at me with ferocity, making me shrink back as I realized how many things that I'd overlooked; how many things I hadn't thought of. "You're the one with the target on your back – the one that people are risking their lives to watch out for. I've been driving this road for hours because I lost you back in the forest, and I knew you'd get here eventually."

"So you were following me," I said, stating the obvious.

"Of course I was, it's my job." He took a deep breath, calming himself down as he nodded back to his car. "Now hop in."

"And if I say no, what are you going to do? Stick me with a sedative again?"

My question was posed to be sarcastic, but as the words left my lips, I realized that it was a definite possibility. Beckett didn't nod or agree, his features staying completely neutral as he said, "I'm not using force this time." He paused a moment. "Please, just get in the car."

The politeness in his voice threw me for a loop, and as I stood there staring at him, I realized the faults in my plan. I didn't know where I was, how far away from home I was, or when the Gemini Clan could pop back up, and even though I didn't think I belonged in Division 27, right now, I certainly didn't belong on a roadside freezing my ass off.

Without saying a word, I slowly moved towards the car, and Beckett didn't say a thing as he walked around his side and slid in behind the wheel. The defeat that fell over me caused a lump to form in the back of my throat as I settled into the passenger's seat.

"So," Beckett begun as he started the engine, "What made you think that going out on your own was a good idea?"

I gulped, holding back the tears that welled in the corner of my eyes. "I was going home."

His eyes widened at my statement, and he looked towards me as a flash of pity crossed his features. One of his hands left the steering wheel as he raked it stressfully through his hair. "Aspen," he started carefully, "you don't have a home."

"Maybe not around here," I said, wiping the stray tears from my cheek with the back of my hand, "But I was trying to find my way back to my apartment and – "

"No, that's not what I..." He shook his head and sighed, glancing over at me. "I thought Catherine would've told you, but I guess she was trying to spare you the details."

A wave of dread crashed over me. "What?"

"The Gemini Clan knew where you lived. The night that I took you back to the Division with me, they must've come looking for you." He paused for a moment. "The next night, when another set of agents were sent out to check on your place, it was completely trashed."

"That can't be," I choked back tears. "That's not true."

"It is," Beckett said quietly, his grip tightening on the steering wheel. "If you want, we can drive out there and I can show you."

The offer had barely left his lips before I shook my head vehemently, letting the tears fall freely down my face. "No." I didn't know where we were, and through my blurry vision, I could see the clock on the dash letting me know that I'd been out here for more than three hours. I was tired, and overall, I was defeated. "No," I repeated, resting my head against the car window, "just drive."

"Aspen."

The combination of hearing my name and a repetitive nudge to my left arm caused my eyes to flutter open. My surroundings were ones that I didn't immediately recognize, but as everything came rushing back to me, I noticed Beckett still seated next to me in the car. I didn't remember much after he had turned the car around just after four in the morning, because amidst the silence, it was too easy to succumb to the exhaustion, and I had dosed off.

"We're back at the Division," he said, grabbing the keys before opening his door. "Come on, I'll lead you back to your room."

Nodding, I stayed quiet as I followed him through the garage that he'd parked in. When we stepped onto an elevator, riding up two floors before hopping off into the storage closet in the back of the training barn, I decided now was not the time to bother with questions about how exactly we'd gotten back when there were no visible roads leading off the grounds.

The sun was just beginning to peek through the trees as we walked towards the building, and despite the early hour, there were quite a few people already awake. One of them however, that both of us seemed to notice at the exact same moment, was Catherine, as she sat alone on one of the benches that sat adjacent to one of the back doors.

Both Beckett and I's steps slowed as we approached her, but when I came to a stop, he simply gave her a nod before continuing towards the building, leaving the two of us alone.

She stood up to greet me. "Aspen," she started carefully, but I cut her off before she could continue.

"I know," I said, my voice breaking with emotion as I moved forwards to take a seat on one end of the bench, "it was stupid to run off." I shook my head, looking down at my hands. "Don't worry, it won't happen again."

"I wasn't going to say that," Catherine said, sitting back down, "even though it certainly wasn't the smartest decision, or the safest." Her tone wasn't strict, but rather laced with kindness, as though she truly cared. "I was going to ask if you were alright?"

A dry laugh escaped my lips. "Is it true?" I sniffled. "That the Gemini Clan destroyed my apartment?"

I peeked sideways just as she nodded with confirmation. "It is."

"So what happens now?" I asked with a defeated sigh.

"As soon as I learned that your apartment had been turned upside down, I put a few agents in charge of making sure there was a cover up," she explained, catching my interest as I raised an eyebrow. "We paid out your lease and cleaned up your apartment before your landlord caught wind of the incident, we cancelled your phone plan, and your employer believes that you were a last-minute acceptance for an out of town continuous education program before you start at Boston College in the fall."

My eyes widened with surprise the more she spoke. "You did all of that in a day?"

She lifted the corner of her lips into a lopsided smile. "We're efficient," she said, "but if you need some time to come to terms with everything, by all means, take it."

"I don't know, it's just strange I guess," I replied, releasing a slow breath. "Waking up here yesterday was surreal, and honestly, confusing, but I didn't take it all that seriously. I thought that eventually, in a few weeks, or months, I'd be able to get back to my old life, but now, hearing that I don't have a life to go back to, I guess it's just cementing the fact that this is all real."

Catherine brought her hand up to rest on my shoulder, willing me to look towards her. "Sometimes life throws you a curveball," she said, "and you don't always know what to do with it, but it's your choices that define you after all is said and done." A flash of something unrecognizable crossed her features. "I guess what I'm trying to say is that being here – being a part of Division 27, it's not easy, but you'll adjust, because I can tell that you're a fighter Aspen. And fighters don't give up."

Chapter 5

I n the days that followed, I kept to myself for the most part. I favoured the Grand Hall and my bedroom, as they were places I was left well-enough alone, and when my thoughts began to veer off in a thousand directions, Kira always seemed to be there to take my mind off of everything.

The two of us had sat in on a beginner's French class – for my benefit more than her own, and she'd briefly showed me the labs that she worked in, as well as some of the other tutorials that the younger crowd frequented.

But while the grounds and the dynamic of Division 27 was slowly growing on me, that didn't mean I was happy.

Besides Kira, most of the people didn't spare me more than a calculating look as I passed them in the halls. Catherine and Finn would stop briefly to see how I was adjusting, while Beckett tried his very best to avoid me at all costs.

I was the new girl – the outsider, and the one that didn't belong.

Then there were the times when I was alone – usually at night when I had the company of the darkness to hide my tears, where my mind began to drift to all the things that I'd left behind and how, exactly, my life had come to be like this. Each time I dried my eyes, I'd tell myself that things would get better – that it wasn't possible for things to get any worse, and I thought that if I said those words out loud enough times, then maybe, one day, I'd truly believe them.

The night exactly a week after my midnight escape, I'd gone to bed feeling semi-alright, but had woken up in a fright after having the same nightmare that had led to my attempted fleeing. This time however, I'd tried my best to put my thoughts to sleep and rest, though it didn't do much good. I spent most the night tossing and turning, and had been incredibly irritated when someone had decided that morning was a good one to beat down my door.

Grinding my teeth, I slipped out from underneath my covers. "I'm coming," I grumbled under my breath, "hold your horses."

When I pulled open the door, it wasn't much of a surprise to see Beckett standing there, unimpressed, with his arms crossed. I raised an eyebrow. "Yes?"

"You've got five minutes to get ready," he said, nodding down to the loose pajamas I wore, "and then you're coming with me."

Before I had the chance to object, both due to my lack of sleep and the early hour, he turned on his heel and headed down the hallway. "And what if I don't want to?" I called after him.

He paused for a moment, and I saw the vague hint of a smirk as he threw a glance over his shoulder. "I guess we'll find out soon, won't we?"

I huffed in annoyance as I shut my door with more force than necessary. There was a part of me – a fairly large part, that wanted to say screw it and go back to bed, but the remaining part was actually eager to see what Beckett had in store. I didn't expect anything over the top, especially from him, but even the smallest of insights into how the agents here trained and operated would be enough to spark my interest.

So, against my better judgement, I walked straight passed my bed and into the bathroom, and when Beckett knocked on the door again ten minutes later, I opened the door with a smug look on my face. "You're late."

He rolled his eyes. "I had to check on something, and it took a bit longer than expected" he replied vaguely, moving aside to let me step into the hall. "Let's go."

Following him down the hall, I waited a few moments for him to explain why he'd woken me up, but when he didn't, I took it upon myself to find out. "Where exactly are we going?"

"First we're going to stop by the Grand Hall to pick up breakfast," he explained as we turned a corner and veered away from the housing wing, "and then I'm bringing you to one of the labs."

"You trust me in a lab?" I asked with astonishment, raising an eyebrow.

"Not in the slightest," Beckett replied, and as he glanced sideways at me, I saw a flicker of amusement in his eyes.

My curiosity spiked, wondering why that was where he was taking me, but as we stepped into the Grand Hall, the gazes that immediately landed on me had my mind otherwise occupied. Over the last week, while I'd frequented the hall for food, I'd tended to eat at times when there was less of a crowd, and now, despite the fact that the sun had barely risen into the sky, almost every table was full.

"Does everyone here get up early?" I asked, leaning in closer to Beckett as I dropped my voice to a hushed whisper.

"It depends." He shrugged. "Some people are probably still up from having a night rotation, but yeah, most people like to make the most of the day if they can – especially if they're still climbing the ladder to get assignments."

Nodding in understanding, I did my best to ignore the eyes boring into my back as I grabbed a parfait and a small protein shake from one of the breakfast bars, drawing my eyebrows together as I saw Beckett hadn't grabbed anything. "Aren't you eating?"

He shook his head, tucking his thumbs into the front pocket of his pants. "I ate earlier," he said, nodding his head towards the doors. "Come on, you can eat once we get there."

Although I was curious about how long Beckett had been awake, I didn't question it as I followed behind him, glad to be leaving the packed hall. Beckett, true to his character, didn't speak much as he led me through the small crowds of people making their way around the building to get a start on their day, and when he stopped in front of a large glass door, he typed a five-digit code into the keypad to the side and pulled on the door handle when the light flashed green.

Strolling in behind Beckett, I stopped short when I saw Kira look up from where she sat in the corner, a microscope and two laptops in front of her, appearing slightly shocked to see us. "Hey guys," she greeted slowly.

"Hey," Beckett greeted. "I hope you don't mind, but Catherine wanted Aspen to get more of a feel for what goes on around here, so I thought she could hang around the lab today."

"What?" I asked as my eyes widened and my gaze swivelled towards him. I thought he'd woken up and actually wanted to show me something himself, not watch over me because of the director's orders and drop me off the first chance he got.

And just like that – with no effort at all, Beckett had succeeded in causing a bubble of annoyance to flow through my veins.

"Did you think I had extra time to play teacher for the day or something?" Beckett asked, directing his question towards me, to which I ground out a harsh no before he turned back towards Kira. "So, is it okay?"

Kira's eyes flitted between Beckett and I for a few seconds, but she eventually nodded, a smile pulling at her lips. "Sure, I don't mind," she replied. "Plus, I can use an extra hand or two with some of this stuff."

"Great," Beckett said. "I'll see you guys around."

And with that, he left.

When the door buzzed shut behind him, locking automatically, I let out a frustrated groan. Dropping my food on the empty counter closest to me, I dragged a stool up next to it and sat down in a huff. "He's so fucking annoying."

"Beckett?" Kira clarified, walking over to me.

"You know, I bet he doesn't even have something he has to do. He just doesn't want to deal with me, and I don't get what I did to piss him off so much."

"Maybe trying to run away your first night?" she suggested teasingly, to which I narrowed my eyes and she laughed. "I'm just kidding. It's probably nothing you did – that's just how Beckett is. But as for having something to do, I know he was out most of the night with a few other agents, so he's probably headed to catch a few hours of sleep before he hits the training barn this afternoon."

The annoyance dulled slightly as I raised an eyebrow. "What was he doing out all night?"

Kira shrugged. "Special assignment probably," she guessed. "Around here, if you're not directly involved with something, you're left in the dark unless it's a large mission, and even then, we're only told the bare minimum to stay safe."

"Like the Gemini Clan?"

"Yeah." She nodded. "When activity leading back to the Gemini Clan increased, Catherine held an assembly to let everyone know to always be on the lookout, and then when your name was thrown into the mix, the senior agents were brought into a rotation to watch over you."

"But what about you?" I asked as I ate. "How do you know all of this if you work in the lab?"

A flicker of sadness crossed her features, though it was quickly masked. "I trained as an agent," she said matter-of-factly, "and I spent two years as a junior agent before I made the choice to switch over to lab work. I wasn't cut out for the front of the line work that some agents do, so I thought I could do some good behind the scenes."

I could've pushed further, figuring there was a definite story as to why she'd suddenly switched paths, but I kept my questions to myself as I glanced around the room. It was large – with several work benches and cabinets full to the brim with different handheld gadgets, as well as a wall devoted solely to computer screens that currently looked to be running some sort of code.

"What are you working on?" I asked as my eyes fell on the bench she'd been working at when I'd walked in with Beckett.

"Well I don't know exactly how much I can tell you," she trailed, walking back over to her work station and grabbing one of the laptops, "but I was examining a few of the different concept devices I had put together over the last month to see if they'd be good fits for a project me and a few of the other people are working on." Bringing the laptop over, she scrolled through the beginning of a document she'd created that had basic charts and graphs, as well as a lot of technical observations written in point form. "If you're interested, I could use some help with some of the basics, or I could get you set up with labelling some of our equipment and materials."

"I can help you," I offered quickly, not wanting to do grunt work in a lab this early in the morning, "just show me what you need me to do."

Smiling with encouragement, she ran me through the fundamentals of the work she was doing, though I did notice she left out what exactly these technologies would be used for.

When she brought me over to her work station, pulling up an extra stool, Kira asked if I'd be okay with recording any important information while she did the main analysis – which I was, and then she put me to work. Not wanting to throw me right into the pages of files on her laptop, she brought out a notebook for me to write in, and as the time passed, multiple pages began to fill up with my scribbled handwriting.

After three hours had passed, my hand was beginning to cramp and an ounce of boredom had clouded my mind. It wasn't that the work wasn't interesting – watching as Kira switched out the small devices was actually something I enjoyed, but the lack of energy and movement wasn't my cup of tea. I often found myself eyeing the other people that dropped into the lab, trying to figure out what they were doing before they turned back and headed for the door, none of them staying longer than a few minutes.

"Aspen."

My attention snapped back to Kira as the door to the lab clicked shut for yet another time, and a sheepish smile grew on my lips. "Sorry," I apologized, knowing it wasn't the first time she'd noticed my wavering concentration. "It's just, how do you do this all day?"

The corner of her lip tipped upwards. "You mean work?"

I shook my head. "No." Glancing out the window that over-looked the back courtyard, I watched as several of the agents – old and young, headed towards the training barn. "I mean, how are you able to sit in a lab while almost everybody else is out there training and in the middle of the action?"

"Not every day is like this. Sometimes I'm working on other projects, manufacturing new technology, or dealing with a secure environment," she explained, "and like I said before, the action just wasn't for me."

I waited a few seconds before I allowed my next words to slip through my lips. "But what if it's for me?"

She leaned back from the microscope and turned towards me, her eyebrows drawn together. "What do you mean?"

"This whole week people have been looking at me like I don't belong here – like I'm not good for anything. Even Beckett," I said, gritting my teeth as I said his name, "thought the only place I'd be of any help was here, doing grunt work with you." I sighed, ducking my head. "I know I'm only here as a safety precaution, but at least I'm trying."

"So, what? You're saying you want to train to be an agent?"

I shrugged. "I don't know. I mean, I'm here aren't I?" I'd never had a set path in life – having decided after high school that it was best to just to live paycheck to paycheck and hold down good paying jobs, but this was a chance for me to spread my wings a bit. "I know it's not something that I can just pick up and go with, but even something small, like sitting in with the trainees or learning basic fighting skills would be better than this," I continued, gesturing to the work in front of us. "No offense."

A laugh escaped Kira's lips. "Non-taken."

"And at the very least, I could learn to defend myself better in case I get attacked again."

There was definite skepticism etched into her features. "Okay," she said slowly, "have you talked to anyone about this?"

I bit my lip. "I didn't really know who I could talk to, besides you."

"Well I can't really do much for you," she replied, "but you could always ask Beckett about it."

Rolling my eyes, I said, "Really? All that would do would get him to laugh in my face."

She smirked. "If not him, then I'm sure there's someone else you've been introduced to that you could talk to about it."

Just as I was about to reiterate the fact that there wasn't really anyone else I was comfortable talking to, a loud buzz sounded throughout the room as the door was pulled open. Finn stepped inside, a laid-back smile on his face as he spotted the two of us across the room.

"Hey Kira, do you mind if I take a new comms device? Mine's been acting up for the last couples of weeks since I got stuck out in that rain storm across state."

"Sure Finn," she replied, standing up to head over to one of the locked cabinets on the other side of the room.

Finn however, walked over towards me and leaned back against the work bench next to ours. "So," he started, raising an eyebrow inquisitively, "you're a lab rat now?"

I shook my head, my lips tilting upwards. "Not really, but I kind of got stuck here today helping Kira."

"And if you wanted to leave?" he trailed, flitting his eyes between Kira and I.

"Here's the new device," Kira interjected, handing over a new walkie-talkie and an ear piece as Finn exchanged them for his old ones, "and if she doesn't want to stick around any longer, Aspen's free to go."

He thanked Kira as she settled back into her work before turning back to me. "What do you say?" he asked. "You wanna grab something to eat?"

Glancing quickly to see an encouraging smile settled on Kira's lips, I stood and nodded. "Sure."

With a quick goodbye to Kira, I followed Finn out of the lab and kept up a mindless conversation with him as we headed to the Grand Hall. It was clear that he was one of the more popular agents around here, as he was stopped by people both his age and years older – all wanting a quick word with him as he smiled politely and took it all in stride.

It was more than twenty minutes later when the two of us had finally made it to the Grand Hall, and with not that many people occupying the space, it didn't take long before we'd both filled our trays and headed towards the far back corner.

"So, what have you been up to so far this morning?" I asked, dropping my tray on a free table while Finn took a seat on the other side.

"If I told you, I might just have to kill you," he said, causing my eyes to widen. When he laughed a second later, I relaxed and dug into my salad, realizing he'd been joking. "No, but really, I was getting briefed for a new assignment by one of my advisors, so – "

"You can't talk about it," I finished for him.

"Exactly." He paused. "But I do want to know how you ended up working with Kira in the lab. I thought you'd kind of just been doing your own thing."

"I was," I replied, "but Beckett showed up at my door this morning on Catherine's order, supposedly, and dropped me off there. It's not like I minded much, because I'm friends with Kira, but I'd rather be doing something more helpful."

"Actually, the labs are really helpful in getting us prepped for assignments and developing new surveillance and gadgets for us to use," he countered.

"I didn't mean it like that," I rushed out.

"I know you didn't." His lips turned upwards as my shoulders sagged with relief. "Though if you're looking to do something other than lab work, I could probably talk with one of the advisors for the junior agents and see if they would be willing to help you out."

"Seriously?"

He nodded. "Yeah, if that's what you want."

"That'd be great," I chirped excitedly, my mood instantly lifting.

I noticed his gaze drift sideways and over my shoulder, his eyes lighting up with an idea. "In fact," he started before yelling out a name and lifting his hand to gain someone's attention. Turning my head, I saw that the man he was flagging down was the same one I'd seen talking to Catherine in her office my first day here. As he walked over, I found myself fidgeting in my seat. "Joe," Finn greeted as the man sided up to our table, "this is Aspen."

"Ah yes," the man said, holding out his hand in greeting. "I believe we met briefly last week. I'm Joe Thompson."

"Aspen Rigby."

"Aspen told me that she was interested in getting a bit more involved with the Division, and I thought maybe you could help her out," Finn explained to Joe before casting a smile my way.

"Well, what exactly are you interested in?" Joe asked, directing his question towards me.

"Um, I'm not really sure," I stuttered honestly. "I was in the lab this morning with Kira, but I didn't think I fit in there very well. Are there lessons I can step into that new recruits get taught specifically, like how S.I.C.O is run, and tips to help their covert skills along? Or even learning a new language?"

Joe nodded, seemingly understanding what I was looking for. "There are a lot of things that our new recruits get tossed into right off the bat, but I could probably put together a lighter schedule for you once I have time to talk to some of my colleagues," he said.

"That'd be great," I said with elation,

"Why don't you come by my office later tonight and we can talk things over?" he continued, which surprised me, as I hadn't thought things could be pulled together so quickly. "It's over in the east wing, and if you get lost, just ask anyone and I'm sure they'll show you where it is."

Excitement and thanks filled my voice as I nodded and said, "I'll be there." When Joe was far enough away, I looked back to Finn with my eyes gleaming. "I can't believe that just happened."

The corner of his lips twitched upwards. "You're welcome."

Chapter 6

My expectations had been low when I'd gone to see Joe that night – thinking that he'd do the bare minimum and slot me into a tutorial or two, but I'd been pleasantly surprised.

Once seated in his office, he went through an overview of the entire curriculum that the Division required new recruits to complete before they were put through training. This included being fluent in at least three languages, an intensive knowledge of covert operations and the history of S.I.C.O, as well as weekly physical and mental one-on-one examinations with an advisor. It was a lot, and when my eyes had widened, he had reassured me that nobody expected me to jump right in.

But that was part of the problem – I didn't think anybody would believe that I could do this.

He worked with me for over an hour to draw together a schedule that I would be able to follow for the next couple of weeks. I'd be focusing on learning how Division 27 functioned in the recent years as well as joining the beginner's French class, but what got me the most excited was when Joe had told me he'd talked to Catherine about stepping on as my advisor. It had sounded strange at first, as well as intimidating – having the head of the Division monitoring my progress, but it also meant that I'd be getting trained by one of the best, so I didn't question it much.

That night I'd gone to bed the most content I'd been since I'd arrived, and when the sun rose the next morning, I woke up feeling refreshed and ready for the day.

I was eating breakfast in the Grand Hall when Joe caught up with me and dropped a thick binder in front of me. It was full to the brim of papers, and when I'd flipped it open with curiosity, he'd explained that it was the previous year's records of everything that had gone on behind these walls. The names of new agents, studies on the lab experiments that had been conducted, in-depths reports of closed cases – it was all in there, as well as much more, and it was my job to read through it all and get caught up.

The task was daunting, but after he wished me luck and I finished off my food, I headed back up to my room to get started. The binder was organized chaos; with multiple handwritten pages that were hard to make out, and by the time I left to head down to my French class, I'd barely made my way through the first twenty pages.

By the time the sun had set in the darkening sky, my brain was pounding with the amount of new information it had absorbed. I made notes on how new recruits were normally brought in (either scouted or due to familial ties), but had mainly kept my focus on nitpicking a few of the cases that had been worked on the previous year.

Three murders in the northwest where the guilty party had been a retired government officer, an attack on the first lady and her daughter, and a cross-ocean investigation where a large pharmaceutical company had orchestrated a warehouse that tested unapproved enhancement drugs on animals – and those cases took up only a sliver of the pages I'd been tasked to look at.

As I closed the binder in my lap, I rested my head back against the wall behind me. Sitting in one of the window seats constructed into the hallway outside of the expansive library that this building housed, I let my gaze wander to the courtyard outside. At this time of night, there were hardly many people still up and wandering the halls, unless they were getting ready for a night assignment.

In fact, I was sure it'd been at least a half an hour since someone had walked passed me.

Gazing out into the night, I spotted the light that was spilling out onto the courtyard from the training barn instantly vanish as a pair of agents closed the doors, presumably the last ones down there, and headed inside.

While the rest of the building seemed to be resting, my body and my brain were wide awake. I was antsy, and pairing that with my wandering mind, it made a dangerous combination.

It was clear, just by talking to Joe, Kira, and Finn, and reading through the case files, that while a lot of the work that agents did was mental, an equal amount of effort was physical. I had a strong mind, but my physical abilities were limited. I'd taken a few self-defence classes in recent years, but judging by the way the members of the Gemini Clan had easily fought off my attempts at escaping, it was clear that I still had a lot to learn.

And I couldn't learn anything if I wasn't given the chance.

Double-checking to make sure that the training barn's lights were still off and that weren't any agents hanging around outside, I stood up and headed back up to my room to drop off my binder before circling back and making my way outside. With each step, I felt the need to glance around at my surroundings as an uneasiness washed over me, knowing that somebody might see me and wonder I was doing. When I pulled hard on the sliding door of the training barn, I opened it just enough for me to slip inside.

"Who's there?"

My shoulders stiffened along with every other muscle in my body as I heard the voice call out in the dark. It was nearly pitch black, and with no visibility of my surroundings, I began to think the worst.

When I didn't reply however, I heard footsteps echoing a long distance away from me, and seconds later, the area was flooded with overhead light.

"Aspen?"

Blinking to adjust to the sudden brightness, my eyes finally settled on Beckett's surprised features moments later.

"Beckett?" I questioned in return, raising an eyebrow with curiosity. "What are you doing here?"

His expression fell flat as he raised his wrapped hands, as if they were enough of an answer. "Practicing."

"In the dark?"

He shrugged, walking back over to the punching bag he'd been using. "Sometimes it's better to practice throwing punches without the light," he explained. "You never know what kind of obstacles you'll face in the field, and if you're infiltrating a hideaway space, most of the time they're underground and dark. It's better to be prepared."

In a weird way, his words made perfect sense. If you could learn to fight without using your sight – only your instincts and your other senses, then you could be a highly valuable asset.

"What about you though?" he asked. "Why are you here so late? Not trying to run away again, I hope."

The tail end of his questioning sounded the smallest bit sarcastic, but I brushed it off as I shook my head slowly. "No," I breathed out before biting my lip, wondering if it was a good idea to tell him the truth. After a quick thought, it wasn't a lie that slipped passed my lips. "I was hoping to practice a few things while nobody else was in here."

Beckett's eyebrows scrunched together as his eyes stayed locked on me. "What do you mean? Did you just want to exercise without anyone around, or ...?" Although he trailed off, I knew the unspoken choice was 'or were you trying to learn how to fight without any help?'. When I crossed my arms instead of replying, his gaze sharpened with judgement and I felt as though I was shrinking in fear. He inhaled sharply through his teeth. "Jesus Aspen, you came in here to practice fighting? Do you know how dangerous that is when you've never been taught?"

"I have been taught," I fought back, though my voice wasn't all that strong.

It was loud enough for Beckett to hear however, as a disbelief crossed his features. "Right," he drawled, "by who?"

"Not that it's any of your business," I stated pointedly, "but I've taken self-defence classes before. I just wanted to see if I still remembered any of the moves."

He was quiet for a moment. "Okay," he said, "let's see what you've got then."

My eyes widened as he stepped up onto the matted floor in the center of the barn and waved me towards him. "What, now?" I stuttered.

"Yes, now," he countered, pausing for a moment as he raised an eyebrow. "Why, is that a problem?"

His gaze was challenging, and while my first instinct was to cower away and head back up to my room for the night, I stood my ground. "No," I replied, letting out a slow, yet determined breath. Moving towards him, I tried to appear calm and confident, masking the other emotions that flooded through my mind as I came to a stop with only a few feet separating us.

"Okay," Beckett instructed, positioning himself into a defensive stance by staggering his feet and turning his body, "I want you to try your best to land a hit on me."

Putting one foot in front of the other, I shifted my weight onto my back leg. "Are you sure?" I asked, a teasing tone attached to my words as I struggled to remember the exact punches I'd been taught through self-defence. "I wouldn't want to hurt you."

I noticed his lips pull upwards in a smirk. "Don't worry, you won't."

As soon as the last syllable left his lips, I tried to catch him off guard by moving forward, and with all the strength I could muster, threw a punch aimed towards his arm. Beckett's instincts were quick however, making it look effortless as he shifted slightly and blocked my punch as he swatted my fist away.

Taking a step back to regain my composure, I brought my arms up to block my face before throwing another punch, this time aiming for his jaw. Yet once again, by simply ducking backwards he managed to avoid getting hit.

I tried again and again, aiming for a different spot each time, but it was no use. Beckett was ready for whatever move I made. With one last attempt, I moved as though I was about to throw another punch, but instead, I lifted my leg and kicked it out towards his stomach.

It wasn't him that was caught off guard, but rather myself, when he wrapped a hand around my ankle and swept my other leg out from under me.

Landing with my back pressed against the mat, I felt the adrenaline pumping through my veins as I struggled to regain my breath. "Shit," I gasped.

Beckett took a step closer to me, offering his hand in assistance. "You okay?" he asked, looking a bit concerned as I slipped my hand into his and got back to my feet.

"I'm fine," I nodded, still breathing heavily. "How are you so good at this?"

"I was trained to fight," he shrugged, "Having strength and a good technique are only a small part it, because if you're not able to defend against your opponent and protect yourself, the rest of it is useless. It's all about studying the other person's body language – watching what side their favouring, where their eyes are looking, what their attack patterns are – and then using the things you notice to your own advantage."

"So what you're saying, is that I suck," I said defeatedly.

"You're actually not as bad as I thought you'd be," he replied. "You know how to throw a basic punch and you have a decent amount of power behind your hits, but you do have a lot to learn if you're going to be sticking around here for a while."

Crossing my arms across my chest, I didn't know what to say.

"Here," Beckett continued, taking note of my uncertainty, "let me show you something. Position your feet as if you were about to fight." Although I wasn't sure where he was going with this, I spread my feet to the width of my hips and placed my left foot in front of my right, placing my weight on right. "You're putting most of your weight on your back foot, which minimizes the amount of movement you have," he stated, pointing to my right leg. "It's best to keep your weight centered, and since your right leg seems to be the one you're favouring, make sure to stand on the ball of your foot so you can move quickly if the situation calls for it."

Taking his direction, I shifted slightly, bringing my fists up to a position to strike. "Like this?"

With his eyes on my feet, he nodded, though as he lifted his gaze to examine the rest of my body, he didn't hesitate to correct my form. "Your knees and feet should be aligned and your hips and your upper body should be turned slightly towards the right," he said, pointing out each part of my body and waiting until I corrected my stance to continue. "Also, your right elbow should be tucked in closer to your ribs while your fist should be resting near your jaw."

As I repositioned my right arm, I felt his hand grip my left wrist slightly as he brought my fist out further from my body.

"There," he nodded in acceptance, taking a step back, "now try to hit me again."

Getting comfortable in my stance as he shifted into a similar position, I took in a deep breath, letting it out slowly before I attacked. My moves weren't aggressive, but rather calculated as I tried to land a punch, though it wasn't a surprise that he managed to block my attempts. He was a good fighter – I'd give him that, but with his tips, I definitely felt more in control of my body.

Surprisingly, as my heart rate began to increase, I felt a rush of energy surge through me. Shifting my right foot a few inches, I managed to turn my body and throw one last punch towards Beckett's ribs, feeling my fist graze against his body before he turned and caught my wrist.

His grip loosened as I stepped back, and even though I knew he was going easy on me, I couldn't help the smile that spread across my lips. "I did it," I said, as if in awe that I managed to get passed his defences – if only for a second.

It caught me by surprise to see a genuine smile appear on Beckett's lips. "Good job," he said, though when he took a few steps back, I noticed his expression shift back to one that was lacking any kind of emotion.

In the short time that I'd been at the Division, Beckett and I hadn't been able to agree on much. There was rarely a time where I wouldn't feel a jolt of irritation while in his presence, and any interaction between us seemed to be forced by others – whether that be Catherine, Kira, or fate looking down on us and laughing at our misery.

Tonight, however, while I know he didn't expect to see me, nor I him, our differences seemed to fade away once we'd begun to fight, and the irony wasn't lost on me – that the only time the two of us could be civil around each other was when we were fighting.

Staying where I was as I watched him retreat to the punching bags, he looked back with a miffed expression. "Is there something else you wanted?"

Narrowing my eyes at his disgruntled tone, I was tempted to turn and head back to my room, but my curiosity got the better of me. "How often do you stay late into the night and train?"

I noticed the split second of surprise that crossed his features when my reply wasn't a snappy comeback, but it faded quickly as he shrugged. "Most nights," he replied simply. "Either I'm waiting to be called out an assignment or I'm the last agent here because I like to train by myself – I like the silence."

It wasn't hard to tell that his last words were added specifically for me, and while my instincts were to roll my eyes and let my sarcasm reign, I held my tongue. There was an idea floating around my head, and while on some levels it was crazy, it also required Beckett and me to be on the same page.

"How do you feel about training me to fight?"

His head jerked quickly towards me. "Seriously?"

I nodded with affirmation. While I was sure that my upcoming meetings with Catherine would help strengthen my physical abilities, I highly doubted that she'd starting by teaching me how to fight. Training at night would give me the freedom to progress at my own speed without having everyone's eyes on me, and the fact that I might end up landing a punch or two on Beckett in the future was something that greatly appealed to me.

The creaking of a door caused my reply to stick in my throat however, because as I took a glance at the barn doors, nobody was there.

"Hey guys."

"Finn," I said, surprised as I whirled back around to see him walking towards us from the back corner of the room, "what are you doing here?"

"I just got back," he said, nodding his head towards the door to the storage closet. In a quick flashback to the night I'd tried to escape, I remembered that there was an elevator back there which led to a parking garage. "I should've been back hours ago, but I got a bit held up," he continued, shifting his gaze between Beckett and I. "What about you two, how come you're up so late?"

"Couldn't sleep," I replied easily, "so I thought I'd walk around for a bit, but I didn't think I'd see anyone in here training – the lights were off."

I risked a glance at Beckett to see that while he'd been somewhat closed off just moments ago, he was now worked up with anger. His shoulders were stiff, his teeth were gritted together, his hands were clenched into fists at his side, and his gaze had hardened as he focused on Finn. It wasn't hard to tell that something was off, but as Finn let loose a laugh, I turned back to him with a smile.

"Yeah, he's weird like that," Finn said in a teasing tone, referencing Beckett. "He likes to train in the dark, but most of us know to just steer clear of him in general when he's training."

If it was possible, I could almost sense that Finn's words only succeeded in angering Beckett further, but even with the pent-up aggression pumping through his veins, Beckett stayed silent and didn't say a word.

"Come on Aspen, I'll walk you back to your room," Finn offered, "Beckett needs to prep for his assignment tonight anyways."

"You have an assignment tonight?" I asked Beckett, shocked, and wondering what sort of timeline agents managed to live on if their job required them to be ready to go at all hours of the night.

He nodded stiffly, throwing a quick glare at Finn as he moved passed the both of us towards the front doors. "I'll see you both later," he said gruffly.

Watching him disappear, I felt the air lighten, releasing the tension that had filled the room with Finn's appearance. There was clearly a history between Beckett and Finn – one that didn't seem to be all that friendly, but what the specifics were, I couldn't be sure.

Turning back to face Finn, I noticed the grin on his face as he raised an arm out for me to hold. "Ready?" he asked cheekily.

Pushing any thoughts of the rift between the two men to the back of my mind, I rolled my eyes and smiled, slipping my hand into the crease of his elbow. "Lead the way."

Chapter 7

"**A**re you okay?"

Breathing heavily, I slowed down my pace – reducing my speed to a relaxed walk before stepping down off the treadmill. Grabbing the towel that Catherine offered me, I nodded. "Yeah, that was only two miles," I replied, wiping the sweat from my forehead and the back of my neck. "I could've done another one or two easily."

While the corner of her lips tilted upwards, the concern that had flooded her features didn't disappear. "I'm not saying you couldn't have," she continued, "but I was actually referring to your shoulder. Did you hurt it recently?"

This was only my third physical training session with Catherine, and what I was quick to pick up on was how good she was at noticing the little things – including the fact that my shoulder was currently not up to par. It wasn't a huge injury, but I'd hurt it when I'd been training with Beckett a few nights earlier.

After the night when Finn had showed up and cut my conversation with Beckett short, I waited up later the following night and made my way down to the training barn – once again finding the place deserted, except for Beckett. I think my appearance had confirmed his suspicions as to whether or not I was serious about having him teach me a thing or two about fighting, and though it took a bit of convincing on my part, he'd begrudgingly agreed to help me.

It was an unspoken agreement however, that our late-night training sessions stayed between the two of us. I didn't want anyone trying to stop me from learning what I thought I had a right to know, and I was sure he didn't want it getting back to Catherine, or any other agents, that he was teaching me how to fight.

A few nights a week I was meeting him down in the training barn – when he didn't have other things on his plate, and up until two nights ago, everything had been going smoothly. I was packing a better punch and I was learning to analyze the small tells that helped me land a few hits on Beckett. That was, until I'd aimed a kick at his ribcage only to have him block it, causing me to land hard on my shoulder as I fell to the mat. The pain hadn't been immediate, as it wasn't until the next morning that I'd felt the ache settle in, so deciding not to push my luck, I'd sat out of training last night.

"Just a bit stiff," I said, the lie slipping from my mouth easily as I tried to put Catherine's worries at ease. "I was just trying to stretch it out a bit while running."

She nodded immediately, and while that led me to believe that she didn't suspect anything, I also knew that she was trained to deceive people when necessary.

"If it's still bugging you in a few days, I'd suggest going to the infirmary," Catherine explained. "A few agents developed a healing solution a couple of years back in our labs that fixes a lot of common physical problems our agents seem to have."

My eyes widened. "Seriously?"

She nodded. "It can't fix broken bones or restart your heart, but it does wonders in alleviating tension from your muscles and mending cuts to the skin."

"Good to know," I replied, bringing my left arm up above my head for a moment to stretch out my shoulder. Dropping my arm, I rolled my shoulders as I glanced around at the other machines. "So, what's next?"

Catherine flitted her eyes between my shoulder and my face, her gaze sharp. "Are you sure you want to keep going?"

Even though, like I had expected, she kept me well away from the fighting and sparring in the center of the room the last two training sessions, I wanted to prove to her that I could put in the work. "Of course," I said firmly.

"Okay then," she said, standing up from the bench adjacent to the treadmills and nodded towards the strength equipment, "we'll do some light upper body training and then get you set up to run a few of the training courses."

Nodding, I bent down to grab my water bottle and took a gulp. "Sounds good."

"Good luck tonight," I said, lifting my eyes as Finn stood up from the other side of the table.

We'd met up for a late dinner in the Grand Hall after I'd freshened up from my training session with Catherine, and now, as he smiled back at me, he was setting off to connect with another group of agents who were heading out on assignment.

"Thanks," he said, his smile shifting into a smirk as he continued, "but I won't need it."

I rolled my eyes. "I'll see you tomorrow – if you're still alive."

"I wouldn't joke about that kind of thing around here," he said quietly, his voice low, though his pupils gleamed with amusement as he picked up his tray and pivoted towards the exit. "See you tomorrow," he threw back over his shoulder before disappearing from view.

Shaking my head at his good-natured personality, I finished up the last of my food before following the path Finn had taken out of the relatively empty Grand Hall. It wasn't that unusual – I'd learned over the three weeks I'd been here – for the more important missions to take place over the weekend, which meant that there were significantly less people milling around the grounds that evening.

Thinking I'd use the free time to get ahead in my French lessons, I turned down the hallway that led to the housing wing, but when I bumped into another person as I rounded the corner, my plans were sidetracked.

The younger girl I didn't recognize simply mumbled an apology under her breath as she continued on her way, but as a dull pain shot through my shoulder, I clenched my teeth instead of returning the sentiment. Turning on my heel, I brought my right hand up to massage my shoulder lightly as I made my way towards the infirmary.

Clearly toughing it out this afternoon hadn't been the smartest idea.

The nurse was incredibly friendly when I'd walked in clutching my shoulder, and after a few minutes of poking and prodding, she'd administered me a small dose of healing solution. In addition to instructing me not to aggravate the muscles overnight – as that was when the drug would work its magic, she'd also given me a shoulder sling with a built-in cooling pad to wear until I fell asleep.

Thanking her immensely, I made my way back towards the housing wing, though I didn't get far – bumping into Kira as she left the lab for the night. I hadn't seen much of her as of recent, as I'd been busy with my nose stuck in a book and she'd had her own work to focus on. Plus, even when we did find time to grab lunch or sit and talk, it seemed like we barely had a chance to catch up before one of us was rushing off.

"Hey," she said, surprised to see me, and when her eyes landed on my shoulder, they widened with concern. "What happened?"

"It's a long story," I grimaced, suddenly feeling a mixture of dread and guilt, "and it looks worse than it is."

Kira quirked an eyebrow, holding back her response for a moment as her gaze held steady. "Are you busy tonight?"

"No..."

"Because I've got a bottle of wine stored away that I've been saving, and this," she said, motioning to my injury, "sounds like the perfect opportunity to crack it open."

Tension immediately spilled from my shoulders and a light laugh escaped my lips as I sighed. "That," I said, the prospect of having a relaxed evening with a friend too enticing to pass up, "sounds great."

After stopping off at Kira's room to grab the bottle of wine and a pair of comfier clothes, we continued down the halls until we reached my room, and it didn't take long before the two of us had changed into our pajamas and were seated across from one another.

"Now," she said, crossing her legs as she sat at the bottom of my bed and twisted the cap off the bottle of rosé, "I believe you owe me an explanation."

"Wine first," I said. There were no qualms about the two of us drinking from the bottle, as she took a sip before handing the bottle to me. Tilting the bottle to my lips, I took two sips, enjoying the taste as the liquid moved smoothly down my throat as I handed it back to her and fell back against my pillows. "So, what do you want to know?"

"Let's start with how you got that sling."

"The nurse gave it to me after she gave me a bit of the healing solution that you guys use," I explained with a teasing undertone, knowing that that wasn't exactly what she was asking.

As expected, she rolled her eyes as she took another sip of wine. "I figured that much," she said. "What I want to know is how you hurt your shoulder in the first place. Shouldn't Catherine still be taking it relatively easy on you in your training sessions?"

I pulled the corner of my lip between my teeth as an internal war begun inside my head. "I didn't injure it while training with Catherine," I answered carefully, though as soon as her eyebrows creased and confusion flooded her features, I sighed, resigning to the fact that I was going to tell her the truth. "I hurt it when I was training with Beckett."

With the words processing in her head and a silence drawing out between the two of us, I reached forward to grab the bottle of wine from her grasp, taking another generous sip. "Beckett?" I nodded slowly. "As in Beckett Donovan? The guy that, up until now, I haven't heard you ever say one good thing about?"

"That would be the one," I confirmed.

She blinked once, and then again, but as she blinked the third time, she threw her head back and launched herself into a fit of laughter. Her laugh was loud and shook her whole body, and all I did was watch, slightly amused by the spectacle, taking sip after sip of wine until she regained some measure of control. "Please," she said, wiping the tears of amusement that filled the outer rims of her eyes, "tell me how that situation came about."

"Not much to tell really," I said, but before I could continue, she interrupted.

"I disagree," she mused. "I want to know how two people who can't stand each other seem to be able to train together without killing each other."

"We aren't that bad," I pointed out, lifting the corner of my lips, "but it does help that I get to take my anger out on him a couple nights a week."

Laughter left her lips once again. "Of course it does, but seriously, how did you even get him to agree to help train you?"

I let out a deep breath, contemplating my answer. "You can't tell anyone about this," I said seriously. "Nobody else knows."

"I won't," she promised, suddenly looking intrigued as she brought her fingers up to draw an invisible cross over her heart.

"I guess I don't really know how it happened," I admitted, still not sure of the details myself. "I went down to the training barn around midnight over a week ago, thinking it'd be empty, but he was still there training alone. I tried to convince him that I knew what I was doing, and he ended up showing me a few pointers after he saw that I could barely landed a hit. His advice actually helped a lot. The next night I went back, and even though he wasn't sure about it, he kept teaching me a few things – watching me get better."

"So what," she started, a frown slipping onto her lips as her gaze flitted down to my shoulder, "did he start trying to hit you or something?"

I shook my head fiercely. "No," I protested, "not at all. He's only ever blocked my attacks, but when I landed hard on the mat a few nights ago, I ended up hurting my shoulder. It also didn't help that I still trained with Catherine this afternoon, when I probably should've been taking it easy."

Understanding clouded her features. "She doesn't know Beckett is training you to fight, does she?"

"No, and I doubt she wants me learning to fight at all, but I want to be prepared." My words had a rougher edge to them as I continued – my determination seeping through. "If the Gemini Clan comes after me again, I want to be able to fight."

When Kira didn't respond right away, I had a moment of doubt – thinking that maybe she'd adhere to the rules and tell Catherine what was going on. It would be her choice after all, and there was nothing I could do to take back the conversation we'd just had.

"I won't say anything," she said slowly, and I released a breath of relief, "but I think that you should." I saw her eyes momentarily glint with despair, but it was gone in the blink of an eye – masked as if it hadn't been there in the first place. "Keeping secrets in a place like this is never a good idea."

The way she said it made me believe that there was a reason she seemed so conflicted, but I didn't want to push her to explain. I knew it was probably a smarter decision to tell Catherine the truth, to explain why I wanted to learn how to fight, but the nagging voice in the back of my head kept telling me that she wouldn't understand.

"Can we just agree to disagree?" I asked, willing her to concede and let the subject drop.

A soft smile pulled at her lips as she nodded. "For now," she said, her eyes dropping to the grip I still had on the wine, "if you pass me the bottle."

Laughing, I did so willingly. As the night went on, the conversation between the two of us slipped into one that was much less serious – ranging from how she got recruited into S.I.C.O to funny stories about customers I'd dealt with while waitressing. It was stress-free, and after twenty days of constant uncertainty and skepticism, a chance to unwind that I desperately needed.

"Seriously?" I snorted, hours later as Kira finished explaining a lab mishap that had happened the first month she'd worked there.

"Unfortunately," she admitted with a grimace. Apparently, she'd added the wrong chemical into a medicine the team had been working on for a few months, and even though she'd only contaminated one vial, it had caused a mini explosion within the lab and destroyed the rest of samples. "But in my defence, the two chemicals were the exact same colour and weren't labeled, so how was I supposed to know which one they wanted me to use?"

"You could've just asked," I mused, "but seriously, they still let you work with them?"

She nodded. "They had all the work they'd done up to that point well-documented, so it wasn't hard to start over after everything was cleaned up, but they definitely kept a close eye on me. I actually think it was another month before they let me do anything on my own."

"Well it all worked out in the end, right?"

"Yeah," she replied, "it did."

"And is that the only thing that's gone wrong in the lab?" I asked, quirking an eyebrow.

A smirk grew on her lips as she shook her head. "No, but you'd need a lot more wine to get another story out of me tonight," she teased as she nodded at the empty bottle that rested beside me.

"I'm sure that – "

A series of knocks cut my bantering short.

"Who is that?" Kira asked glancing over her shoulder at the closed door before turning back to me with confusion creasing her forehead.

"I have no clue," I said slowly, pushing myself up from the bed and looking at the clock to see that it was just past midnight. Reaching the door, I pulled it open just enough to catch a glimpse of who was standing there. My eyes grew in surprise as I saw Beckett, his hands tucked into his pockets and a blank expression on his face, and I stepped aside to let him in. "What are you doing here?"

He opened his mouth to respond, but as I let the door close behind him, his eyes fell to my injured shoulder. "What happened?" he asked quietly, and as he raised his gaze to meet mine, I saw the smallest glimpse of concern.

"Oh, um," I stammered, "nothing really."

"She hurt it a few nights ago training with you."

Kira's voice caused the both of us to turn her way – me with narrowed eyes and Beckett with tense shoulders, as up until that moment, he believed the two of us were alone. She raised an eyebrow at us, though she kept quiet, completely content with watching the conversation play out between Beckett and I.

"Is that true?"

"I'm fine," I stressed, giving Kira a pointed look before turning back to Beckett. "I went to the nurse and she gave me some of the healing solution you guys use, so I'll be good as new in no time."

"And that's why you didn't show up yesterday, or tonight?" he asked, his voice low. I nodded. "Why didn't you say something?"

I ducked my head as a mixture of guilt and embarrassment clouded my mind. "I didn't want you to think that I couldn't handle learning how to fight," I admitted apologetically. "This isn't your fault. I wanted to learn how to fight, so I have to deal with the injuries that come with that."

A conflicted set of emotions crossed his face as he raised his right hand and dragged it stressfully through his jet-black hair. It was as though he wanted to say something – the words on the tip of his tongue, but something was holding him back. I waited for him to respond, and as the seconds ticked by with nothing but silence, I began to get antsy.

Beckett's reply never came however, because the moment I thought he'd finally speak up, he took a step away from me. Turning on his heel, he pulled open the door and left, letting it fall shut behind him with a loud thud.

Left staring at the door with an open mouth and disbelief etched into my features, I felt a strong wave of confusion wash over me.

"Well," Kira started, and I turned back to face her, "that was interesting."

"Yeah," I trailed in agreement, wondering what the hell had just happened, "it was."

Chapter 8

Two nights later, after giving my healed shoulder an extra day of rest, I was back in the training barn with Beckett, and he was back to his usual broody self.

"Come on," he said, standing behind me and egging me on, "keep it up. Punch harder and remember the combination."

My fists were moving in rapid succession as I repeated a training combination against one of the speed balls – working my upper body and muscle memory as I held my feet shoulder width apart. I'd gotten a hang of the rhythm quickly – right, right, left, left, repeat – but as my arms began to tire and sweat started to pile up in the gloves I wore, I gave the bag one last punch before taking a step back.

"Tired?" Beckett asked, crossing his arms over her chest and raising an eyebrow as I turned his way.

Shaking my head, I bent down to grab the water bottle I'd brought down with me. "Just needed some water," I replied, slowing down my breathing as I took long gulps, "but just wondering," I continued with curiosity, "are you purposefully giving me solo drills so that I won't have to fight you?"

It'd been nagging me for the last thirty minutes, as he'd moved me from one apparatus to another, that he was holding back because he knew that I'd hurt myself a few days back. I was fine – which I'd told him flat out when we'd started tonight, but from the way his shoulders tensed momentarily, it was clear he was treating me with precaution.

"I knew it," I said accusingly, before he could deny it, "you don't think I can handle it."

"It's not that – "

"I don't know what misconceived notion you have in your head, but I'm fine," I stressed, pulling off my gloves and dropping them to the floor as a stream of anger began to pulse through my veins. Walking with heavy footsteps towards the center of the room, I turned back to face Beckett with my hands on my hips. "So... are we going to train for real, or are you going to keep treating me like an invalid?"

His stubble-covered jaw twitched with annoyance, but he fought back against the wariness that filled his mind by stepping up onto the mat.

"Good choice," I said, limbering up as I shifted my weight from side to side.

Once he was about a foot away from me, I moved into my defensive stance, and when he did the same, I didn't waste a second before going on the attack. I punched my right fist forward, aiming for his chin, though it was easily dodged as he leaned back and awaited my next move. My next few punches came with similar results - him dodging expertly as I threw my all into trying to land a hit.

The anger within me built up with each hit that he successfully avoided, and a will to show him exactly what I could do washed over me.

Moving forward, I purposefully left my guard down as I swung a fist towards his face, and when he ducked, lightly tapping the opening I'd given him, I lifted my knee towards his stomach. However, my plan didn't work out quite as I'd hoped. Just as my knee met his ribcage, he grabbed a hold of my leg and pulled slightly, throwing me off balance and sending me hard down onto the mat.

The air whooshed out of my lungs and I struggled momentarily to regain my breath.

"Are you okay?" Beckett asked, leaning over me as he offered me a hand. Accepting the help, I managed to nod as I made my way back onto my own two feet, albeit rather wobbly. "Because if you're not, we can stop for the night."

"We don't need to stop," I wheezed, frustration seeping in as I drew in a breath and slowly released it, "I'm fine."

"Aspen," he said carefully, "you don't need to push yourself."

My fists tightened at my sides. "Yes I do," I replied, my voice low and steady, "because if I don't – " I gulped, unable to continue as the alternative settled into my mind.

"What? What is so important that you're willing to hurt yourself?"

"Because if I can't handle fighting you," I started, my voice cracking as I lowered my gaze, "how am I supposed to be able to hold off the Gemini Clan?"

I heard a heavy sigh leave his lips, though my eyes stayed glued to floor. "That's what all this is about?" he asked, and I nodded slowly. "Fuck, Aspen. Seriously? I thought you just wanted to get ahead in your training, not go chasing after the impossible."

"I – "

There was nothing I could say to defend myself however, as my voice was quickly overpowered by Beckett's. "I can tell you right now that you won't be able to match up to the agents of the Gemini Clan." His words did nothing if not cut at my confidence. "You're here for a reason – to stay safe, and if you ever tried to fight back against the Gemini Clan, it wouldn't last long. You can train all you want, but these people, they're faster, they're stronger, and they don't care if you get hurt in the process."

My shoulders were tight as I tried to hold myself together, though I couldn't help but flinch at the aggression attached to his words.

"Once you get that through your head – that fighting isn't about winning, but having the strength to put yourself in danger to help someone else, then maybe I can help you." He shook his head, his words quieter and filled with protest. "But right now, I can't."

My breath hitched as he took several steps backwards, drawing away from me before he turned on his heel and didn't look back. Confusion flooded my mind, but as I sank to the mat, circling my arms around my knees, I could feel the pain slowly seeping in – more prominent than anything a physical injury could ever bring.

That night was restless, and as I laid awake in bed, Beckett's words danced through my head on a repetitive loop.

You won't be able to match up to the agents of the Gemini Clan.

They're faster, they're stronger, and they don't care if you get hurt.

Unable to shut off my brain, I ended up tossing and turning for hours before I finally managed to fall asleep around three in the morning. Though when I awoke bright and early the next morning, the remains of tears stained my cheeks. In an effort to rid the distress from my features, I jumped in the shower and let the spray fall over me, hoping that it would wash away more than just the tears, but my thoughts as well.

As the day passed, I managed to keep myself busy with other tasks - from paying attention in my French lesson to having lunch with Finn and stopping by to see Kira. When my distractions ran out however, I found myself alone, isolated in my room as I flipped through the last of the closed cases from the previous year.

Unfortunately, a majority of them revolved around the Gemini Clan.

It seemed as though whispers of the Gemini Clan growing stronger had begun in late October, and once their name was out there, they hadn't seen the point in hiding in the shadows. At first, it had started out with unexplained breaking and entering charges and government databases being hacked for personal information, but no one had been able to figure out who was responsible.

They had covered their tracks well, but then they'd made one small mistake – they'd pulled up my information on the government databases.

As my eyes latched onto my name scrawled across the bottom of the page, I froze. Noting that the entry was from the beginning of December, I quickly read it over again, and again, making sure that I hadn't made a mistake or misunderstood.

But I hadn't. It was my name that had alerted Division 27 of the Gemini Clan's activity.

My mind raced and I couldn't understand how I was connected to all of this, but all I could do was keep reading. I didn't want a half-assed reply to the questions I was dying to ask – I had to know the truth.

Every report following was related to work the Division was doing to stop the Gemini Clan, and after rereading them multiple times, the handwritten words were firmly ingrained into my mind.

Stepping up from simple hacking and breaking and entering, they'd moved on to abducting and torturing high-profile citizens that were privy to highly classified information. The Division had caught on quickly that the previously hacked files belonged to each of the victims of abduction and had put their best agents on surveillance to intercept the attacks.

For some, the protection had worked, but others weren't as lucky.

When the clock had struck midnight on the 31st of December, a total of four victims had been killed at the hands of the Gemini Clan after refusing to give up vital security information or knowledge pertaining to classified research experiments. The agents belonging to Division 27 had been unable to gather enough intel on what exactly the Gemini Clan was after, and during their efforts, two agents – a man and a woman, had been killed while out on assignment.

Flipping the binder shut, I didn't know what to think. On one hand, this binder had contained everything I had asked for – more information about what this place was and what exactly the agents worked so hard for, but on the other hand, it'd left me more confused than I'd been in the first place. I'd thought reading this would give me answers, but instead, all I had was more questions.

When I finally pulled myself out of my head, I realized it was late. The sun had already set beyond the trees and the darkening sky had begun to glow with stars as they appeared one by one.

I'd managed to skip dinner – far too immersed in my reading, and while I knew there would still be some food leftover in the Grand Hall, I didn't think I was capable of holding much down. My mind was too scattered, and every thought linked back to the Gemini Clan, causing the pit of my stomach to fill with unease. When my leg began to shake – a nervous tick I hadn't known I possessed, I knew I couldn't stay holed up in my room for the remainder of the night, no matter how much I wanted to.

Hoping fresh air would do me some good, I swung my legs over the side of my bed and headed down the hall, stepping out into the cool night air minutes later. Crossing my arms across my chest in an attempt to fight off the wind, I made my way along the path that lead towards the forest that surrounded the Division. It was the same walk I'd taken my first night here – the night I'd tried to leave, but this time, I stayed. As I reached the trees, I turned and walked along the line, making my way slowly around the grounds and occasionally weaving in and out to keep myself in the shadows.

My movements were mindless as the words I'd read stayed at the forefront of my thoughts. It wasn't something I could forget easily – the fact that my name alone could clue this Division into the Gemini Clan's actions. I knew there was more to the story that hadn't been recorded; there had to be. However even after three laps of the grounds, I was still unable to come up with a plausible explanation.

My frustrations grew with each step I took, and after rounding the grounds once more, I turned to head back inside, only to stop short when I noticed Catherine standing there. She nodded and greeted the other agents who passed, but as an unsettling feeling settled over me, I had a gut feeling that she was there to see me.

Continuing towards her, the desire to flee and avoid an inevitable conversation coursed through me, but I pushed it down, knowing that, while I might not like what I'd hear, I had to know the answers to the questions circling my head.

Mainly, how I was linked to the Gemini Clan.

"I could see you weaving through the trees from my office," she said, nodding towards the tree line behind me and con-firming what I already knew – that she was here to talk to me. "Wanted to check on you; make sure that I wouldn't have to send an agent out looking for you again."

I shook my head, managing the briefest of smiles despite my nerves. "No, I wasn't running away," I said, "just thinking."

"Anything I could help with?"

Biting my lip, I nodded. Sitting down on one of the benches that lined the walkway, waiting to speak until she did the same, watching me with a curious expression. "I finished the binder that Joe gave me," I started, my voice quiet, yet thick with emotion.

Understanding filled her eyes before they clouded over with an unrecognizable emotion. "I see."

"Everything was so intense at the end of last year," I trailed off, my heart squeezing painfully at the thought of two of her agents being killed on duty, "but what am I missing? What happened after everything settled?"

"We regrouped," she said, as though the answer was simple. "It was a new year and we needed a new mindset after losing two of our top agents. The Gemini Clan was stronger than we thought, and we were forced to reach out and get support from a few other divisions. Now we have three other divisions – 4, 19, and 25, helping with the on-going investigations."

I gulped. "And have you gotten any closer to taking them down?"

Although I expected the answer, it didn't hurt any less when Catherine sighed and shook her head. "No, unfortunately, we haven't," she replied. "Since we lost agents late last year, we've been careful with sending out agents on direct assignments unless they're absolutely needed – like when we had agents tailing you."

"But that's what I don't understand," I said with frustration, my fists tightening to the point where my fingernails bit into the skin of my palm, "how am I connected to all of this in the first place? Why did my name alert your agents that the Gemini Clan was behind everything that had happened last fall?

She dropped her gaze, almost nervously, as she replied. "My agents didn't figure it out – nothing about your name would've been triggering for them. It's just another name among many."

My eyebrows creased. "Then how – "

"I was the one who made the connection."

"You?" I asked, astonished. "But, how?"

"I've been a part of S.I.C.O for a long time – I grew up here," she replied, detaching her emotions from her words. "I was able to figure out who you were, and it wasn't long before I made the connection between you and the Gemini Clan."

"What connection?" I asked, begging for a straightforward answer. "What did they want with me? How did they know who I was? "

This didn't make any sense. I had no connection to Division 27. To S.I.C.O. Not unless –

My eyes widened, and seeing the realization sink into Catherine's features that I had figured it out, I knew that the track my thoughts had turned onto was the right one. "My parents?" I asked, my voice thick with disbelief.

Catherine nodded slowly.

This confirmation sparked a whole new pile of questions. "Who are they then?" I asked in a rush, and when she didn't respond right away, I continued. "Are they still alive? Did you know them?"

She gulped, and instead of appearing as the confident woman I knew her to be, she looked incredibly skittish and unsure of herself. "They're still alive," she finally replied after a prolonged silence, "and I... I knew your father."

"Well if you knew my father, you must've known who – "

No.

No – it couldn't be.

But no matter how many times I tried to push the thought out of my mind, I couldn't help but focus on the way she averted her eyes and the way her shoulders tensed up as I went silent. There was no denying it – she knew what I had figured out.

When her gaze finally lifted to meet mine, my throat went dry as I noticed all the little things I had never thought about before. Her hair – how it was the same dark shade as my own. The way her nose curved slightly to the left like mine did, and while I didn't have the same colour eyes, I saw a resemblance in her that I saw every time I looked in a mirror.

I didn't even need to say the words, because deep in my heart, I already knew that it was true.

Catherine Sommers was my mother.

Chapter 9

"You're... you're," I stuttered, unable to get the words out. I watched through tear-filled eyes as she nodded slowly, and I released a strangled breath. "But... how?" I choked out.

She turned her gaze away from me. "I had been seeing your father for about a year before we went our separate ways," she started, her voice thick with emotion. "I was already a senior agent by then, and when I found out I was pregnant, I was devastated."

Her words cut straight through the walls I'd built up over the years as the tears in my eyes began to fall.

"It wasn't something I had ever wanted, and since I found out after your father and I were separated, I never told him," she admitted. "The pregnancy was hard, but I wanted to do the right thing. I set up a closed adoption so that I knew you'd be safe, but when you were born, there was a moment when I thought about raising you myself. You were so small and beautiful," she said, getting choked up as she turned back to face me, "but I couldn't do it. I knew that for you to have a normal life, you'd need to do that away from me."

"So you let me go," I stated point-blank.

"Yes," Catherine whispered

"How did you even know my name then?" I asked, a painful lump growing in my throat. "If it was a closed adoption, you shouldn't have known."

"Your parents told the nurses they were okay with me knowing, so before I left the hospital, I was told that my daughter's name was Aspen Rigby."

"And you never thought to look for me?" I asked, anger quickly overtaking my initial shock.

"Of course I did," she replied immediately "but with this job – working at S.I.C.O, I knew it wasn't safe for you."

"It wasn't safe for me here?" A dry laugh escaped my lips, my words accompanied by a hard edge. "Were you ever notified that my adoptive parents – my real parents, died in a car crash when I was eight years old? That I was put into the foster system and forced to fend for myself most of the time? That's not what I'd call living a safe life."

"Aspen..." she breathed, a pained expression crossing her features.

"No," I said aggressively, shaking my head as I stood up, "I don't want to hear it. You made your choice, and now I'm making mine."

Ignoring the way my chin trembled and my chest ached, I turned on my heel and walked away. Catherine called out for me to wait – to let her explain, but her words fell on deaf ears. My steps became faster and more purposeful as I reached the building, and as I moved through the halls towards my room, my hair fell to shield my face and my tears fell hard.

By the time I let my door fall shut behind me, I barely had the strength to carry myself to the bed, collapsing just as I reached it. My breaths were shallow and I felt light-headed, too many emotions trying to push themselves to the forefront of my mind.

It was suffocating.

I'd been given exactly what I wanted – an answer to the questions that had burned my curiosity, and while I knew Catherine's admission had been honest, I was left unsatisfied.

More questions circled, and as I curled up alone, I could feel myself falling deeper into the rabbit hole.

It was the first time since I'd arrived at Division 27 that I'd slept long into the afternoon.

My emotional and mental limits had been shattered and my body was exhausted – as though the truth of who I was had drained any ounce of strength I had. Not once had I woken up after closing my eyes the night before, laying dreamless in the comfort my bed brought me until the sound of a sharp crack of thunder forced its way through my skull.

It seemed fitting that the weather reflected my mood – the thunder a rumple of anger in the sky, the rain a downpour of sadness, and the lightning a jolt of surprise. The storm was violent and unexpected, casting dark shadows over the grounds as the howling winds picked up speed.

They said things got better after a storm, but in that moment, I wasn't sure if I believed it.

Bleary eyed, I felt a headache begin to pound as a result of the tears that had been shed as I'd slept, staining my cheeks and leaving my eyes rimmed red. It would've been easy for me to stay in bed the rest of the day and act as though I'd fallen ill, but I couldn't let myself appear weak. Instead, I lifted myself up – showering and getting dressed as I felt the walls that had been torn down build themselves back up.

The halls were busier than usual as I headed towards the Grand Hall, everyone confined inside the building and un-willing to brave the weather. I couldn't help but glance at each person I passed, wondering who all knew of my con-nection to S.I.C.O, and who'd been left in the dark just as I had.

Did the senior agents know? Did Kira? Finn? Beckett? Did everyone know?

I felt as though my composure was hanging by a thread, dangling me over the edge of a cliff. My posture was stiff; my shoulders tense as I fell in line to grab a small salad and a bowl of fruit. It was when a hand came down on my shoulder however, that I jumped, spinning on my heel with wide eyes only to see Kira standing there, a slightly amused look on her face.

"Whoa, sorry," she said, a bit of laughter spilling from her lips, "I didn't mean to scare you."

I let out a slow breath. "Don't worry about it," I replied, shrugging it off, "I'm just a little on edge because I haven't been feeling all that well this morning."

Her forehead creased as she bought the lie, flitting her eyes towards my shoulder. "I thought your shoulder had healed?"

"It did. It's more a headache that's bugging me than any-thing else."

"Oh, hopefully you're feeling better soon," she said, "and if you want somewhere quiet to hang out, the lab is pretty sound proof. I've been working there alone the past couple of hours, so I'm sure no one would mind if you wanted to come and do some reading or something."

Her words sounded genuine, though I couldn't help but wonder if she knew about my relationship to Catherine and was simply keeping it from me. After all, she'd been an agent once, and on top of the fighting, it'd been her job to be able to mask her emotions and gather intel by lying and being deceitful.

Just as I was about to respond, my gaze drifted over her shoulder to see Catherine walking into the Grand Hall, her eyes landing on me immediately. "Sorry," I said in a rush, pushing my way past Kira as I headed towards the exit, "I've got something I have to do."

It was another lie, but I couldn't face Catherine. Not yet.

Knowing she wouldn't be able to follow me without raising suspicion, I quickened my pace, but instead of heading back to my room, where I knew she would easily be able to find me, I made my way towards the library. Bypassing the rows of tables near the entrance that seemed to be full of agents hiding out as the storm blew over, I made my way towards the back of the room. I'd never been through the stacks before in fear of getting lost, but in that moment, it was exactly what I wanted. To get lost and to be left alone.

Eventually, after weaving my way through the numerous pathways, I made it to the back entrance, which consisted of a large glass pane that was getting pelted with rain and a door that led outside to an enclosed gazebo. From what I could tell, it was completely empty, and without much thought, I pushed open the door and ducked my head, making a sprint through the rain.

Pulling open the flimsy door, I stepped inside, pushing my damp hair back from my face as I took in the small space. It was isolated on the far-right side of the grounds and could probably only hold a maximum of six people, but it was cozy as I sat down on one of the benches, pulling my knees to my chest. The heavy rain was a calming sound as it beat down on the roof of the gazebo, but no matter how hard I tried, as the minutes of silence ticked by, the rumbles of thunder and the brief flashes of lightening couldn't drown out my thoughts.

It was a shadowed figure moving towards the gazebo that pulled me out of my head and sent a jolt of panic through my veins. They were tall, but with the rain picking up, I couldn't see much. It could've been anyone – Catherine, another agent, or...

Someone else.

My arms tightened around my legs as the person moved closed and I mentally counted the seconds I had left to myself. Three. Two. One.

Even though I'd realized he had a talent for showing up at times when I least expected, I was still surprised to see Beckett step inside the gazebo, a rush of cool air following close behind him. His hair was still dripping, sticking to his forehead before he ran a hand through it to push the strands away from his face, and the rest of him seemed just as soaked.

"How did you know where I was?"

"I didn't," he replied simply, "but Kira came to see me, wondering if I knew what was going on with you. She said you were on edge when she saw you earlier. Plus, this light," he pointed to the dim lantern that hung from the center of the ceiling, "casts a pretty heavy glare through the rain."

"Great," I muttered under my breath, ducking my head down to my chest. "Well you have nothing to worry about, I'm fine."

"You know you aren't that great a liar," he pointed out, his hands finding their way into the pockets of his trousers.

His bluntness was unwelcomed, especially after two nights ago in the training barn, when he'd been brutally honest with me about my lack of skills and the impossible mission I seemed to be on to fight back against the Gemini Clan. I hadn't seen him since, and I hadn't yet built up the strength to talk to him again, let alone listen.

"What do you want?" I asked, my voice thick – just above a whisper.

The silence that followed was long – and for a moment I questioned whether he'd changed his mind and wanted to turn around and step right back into the storm. When he took two steps towards me however, taking a seat on the other end of the bench, I knew he wasn't leaving until I heard him out.

"I had a meeting with Catherine the morning." With my feet now planted on the floor and my gaze still directed downwards, now focusing on the way my hands clenched together on my lap, I didn't have to look up and see his expression to know what was coming next. He knew – and for how long, I had no idea. "It seemed like all she wanted to talk to me about was you."

"Did she order you to follow me around and keep an eye on me?" I sneered. "Because if it'll make her feel better, you can tell her that I'm not stupid enough to leave – not again."

There was a pause, as though he didn't know how to respond.

"You know she only wanted what was best for you."

My chest felt heavy as I lifted my head slightly, looking over at him through my lashes, ignoring his statement for a moment as I asked the question that was bothering me the most. "How long have you known she was my mom?"

He met my gaze as he replied. "Since last year, when she assigned me to be one of the agents watching out for you." I released a staggered breath, fearing that was the case. "Everyone who'd be assigned to tail you knew, but once I brought you back here, word spread."

I gulped. "So everyone...?"

"Everyone knows," he confirmed, "but it was Catherine's idea to keep you in the dark until you needed to know. Like I said, she wanted what's best for you."

"If she was worried about my well-being, she would've told me the truth the minute I met her," I responded roughly, my anger beginning to bubble back up to the surface. "She wanted me far away from this place, and she failed, because even after all her attempts at keeping me a secret, I still ended up here."

"I don't think you're giving her enough credit."

My eyes narrowed and surprise filled my features. "Seriously?" I grinded out. "She was afraid of her past coming back to haunt her – that's all."

"She was afraid of you getting pulled back into his life, the one that she tried so hard to keep you away from." My mind was screaming at me to cut him off – to tell him I didn't want to hear it, but the words wouldn't come. Maybe on some level, I did want to hear what he had to say. "Catherine might not have made the best choice when she gave up, but at least she was able to make a choice."

I didn't know where he was going with this, and as I glanced over at him with my eyebrows drawn, I saw that his eyes were fixed forwards, his hands clenched by his sides.

"My parents were double agents," he admitted. "They were part of the Gemini Clan and too scared to leave, but they helped to source intel to S.I.C.O whenever they could. As a kid, they left me out of their work and I stayed with a babysitter while they were out on assignments. At the time, I didn't know what their job was – I only found out after, but I was old enough to know that they were choosing their job over spending time with me."

Maybe it was the way his voice lacked emotion, or the way his Adam's apple bobbed, or just the overwhelming amount of information that had passed through my head in the last twenty-four hours, but I felt a lump form in my throat and a wetness gather in the corner of my eyes.

"One night when I was eight, they were both called out on a last-minute assignment. I was already asleep, and they thought they'd be back before I woke up, so they didn't call a sitter." I saw his knuckles turning white as his fists clenched tighter. "I woke up a few hours later, and I was alone. It was your mom that ended up finding me two nights later." My breath hitched. "The Gemini Clan hadn't known I existed, but a few S.I.C.O agents had. My parents wanted me to be safe if anything had ever happened to them, so after they died... I was brought into Division 27 at the request of Catherine."

I flinched when I felt Beckett's hand cover my own as it laid on the bench beside me. His skin was still cold from the rain, but as I waited for him to gather the rest of his thoughts, I didn't move my hand away.

"At the time, she'd been a senior agent for years already, and was working her way up the ranks – mentoring the new recruits and guiding them through training. I was alone and by far the youngest person inside these walls, but as I kept to myself in the room I'd been given, Catherine always came to check on me." He finally turned towards me, an intense honesty gleaming in his eyes behind the glassy wall of tears. "She watched out for me as I grew up, and pulled me away from what could've been a totally different ending."

After several seconds of silence, I knew he'd said all he could, yet there wasn't much I could say in response. I wasn't used to this Beckett – the one that was willingly opening up instead of keeping everyone at a distance. It felt like he'd purposefully let me into his past – his pain – to lessen the pain that I was feeling.

"My parents died when I was eight too," I said, his honesty prompting my own as my gaze once again shifted downwards so that my chin touched my chest. "Car crash."

"I'm not making up excuses for her, it's just," he sighed, "it wasn't easy growing up as a child surrounded by things I had no business knowing about. I didn't really get a normal childhood, and I think that's one of the reasons why she felt putting you up for adoption was the right choice."

"Jumping around from one foster home to another isn't what I'd called an ideal childhood either," I pointed out, my voice quiet, with much less anger attached to my words.

"I know," he admitted, "and I'm not arguing with that, but you were able to go to school, make friends with people your own age, and grow up not having to worry that there was danger around every corner – I never had that."

I could understand where he was coming from. It was easy to see that the way he'd been raised reflected his actions now – how he kept people at a distance, how he tried his best to stick to the rules, and how he spoke the truth, no matter how hard it was to hear.

"I can't just put everything behind me," I said, a hiccup in my voice, "I can't forget that she gave me up and she tried to hide the fact that she's my mom."

"And I'm not asking you to," he replied, squeezing my hand. "I just wanted you to know that Catherine is a good person. We all make mistakes we have to live with – choices that haunt us every day, but she does want to talk to you; when you're ready."

I nodded, unable to formulate a response. Instead, with both of our minds filled with a complicated stream of thoughts and emotions, the two of us sat there in silence, not moving away from one another until the rain let up and the sun peaked out from behind the clouds.

Chapter 10

The crashing waves that my emotions had been riding slowly began to settle as the days passed. It was strange – knowing that after all these years I did have a family. A mother. However, no matter how many times we passed each other in the halls or locked eyes across a sea of people in the Grand Hall, I couldn't muster up the strength to do more than give her an acknowledging nod.

It was clear that others had picked up on the tension between the two of us, namely Kira and Finn, who had seen me duck out of sight on more than one occasion when Catherine was around. They'd both confronted me, and though I'd been honest in telling them that I knew, I was also clear when I said that I wasn't ready to talk about it. I knew they were concerned and had questions, but they kept their thoughts to themselves, for which I was appreciative.

A side effect of ignoring Catherine however, meant that my training schedule had been shattered to pieces. I knew I didn't have the capability to listen to her instructions and work with her while things sat as they did, and because of this, I'd been skipping both our in-class and physical training sessions. My other option had been Beckett, but he wasn't talking to me. Not since the conversation we'd had in the gazebo, and with the way we'd left things before that, I was on the fence about reaching out to him at all.

However, not wanting to sit back and do nothing, I took matters into my own hands.

Standing outside of Joe's office, I knocked; waiting until I heard his voice inviting me in to push open the door and step inside.

"Aspen," he said, slightly surprised as he hadn't expected me, "What brings you here?"

"I finished reading through the binder you gave me," I said, my words hesitant as I slid the binder out from under my arm and onto his desk.

He nodded, casting an expectant look towards me. "And I'm assuming you have questions?"

"I did," I took a deep breath, exhaling slowly, "but Catherine cleared a lot of things up for me."

"Okay," he drawled, clasping his hands together atop his desk, "then what can I do for you?"

"I was wondering – " I paused for a moment, trying to think of the best way to phrase my next words. " – if you had any time over the next couple of weeks to fit me into your training schedule, or find somebody else that could." I bit my lip, watching as his forehead creased with confusion and knowing I'd have to further explain. "Things aren't really working out with me and my mom."

"Ah," he said, understanding flashing in his eyes as he leant back in his chair, "I'm guessing she told you."

I nodded, subconsciously replaying the events of my conversation with Catherine in my mind. Unable to sit down due to a rush of restlessness, I walked to the side of his office, running my fingers over the books that lined the shelves. Some were classics, like Sherlock Holmes and Casino Royale, while others were clearly job specific. Titles like Disarming Bombs and other Explosives and The Art of Tailing fell under the latter category, and with defined creases in the spines, they appeared to be well used.

"You know she volunteered to train you for a reason," Joe continued, realizing after a prolonged silence that I wasn't going to reply. I turned towards him, attempting to appear unbothered, but with the way I shifted constantly from one foot to another, I knew I wasn't pulling it off. "She hasn't been directly involved in training new recruits for years now."

The corners of my lips pulled upwards, though it was more due to an uneasiness that flowed through me than a feeling of happiness. "Which should've been my first clue that something was up," I pointed out. "She only wanted to train me because she knew I was her daughter – which apparently, everyone else knew too."

"Now, I'm not denying that I knew about the relationship between you and Catherine, but it wasn't my place to tell you, nor was it anyone else's but Catherine herself," he said. "She didn't want you to be overwhelmed with this, on top of dealing with the stress of leaving the comfort of your old life behind. That being said," he paused, the serious tone in his voice morphing into something softer, "I am glad she's told you."

"She's my mom," I said, aware of the nod of confirmation he gave as I stated what the both of us already knew, "but I haven't been able to talk to her since I found out. I just... I can't think of anything to say."

"I'm sure it's not easy, being thrown another curveball," he replied, "but if you don't think you can handle working with her right now, I'll talk to Catherine. I'm sure that we can work something out so you can train with me until you're ready to set things straight with her."

I released a breath of relief, my chest feeling lighter as I said, "Really?"

Joe nodded. "Just know that the longer you put the conversation off, the harder it's going to be."

Sighing, I knew he was right, but this wasn't something that could be talked through and then pushed aside. Once everything was out in the open, there was no going back, and that wasn't something I was ready to face just yet.

"How was your lesson with Joe?" Kira asked a few days later as I walked into the lab. She stepped back from the experiment she was working on, pushing her safety glasses up onto her head, and waiting as I dropped my stuff on the table at the front.

"It was okay," I replied, taking a seat far enough away from her out of fear that I'd unknowingly interfere with her work. "He went over a few qualities that a good agent should have – "

"Let me guess," Kira cut in, "intuition, intelligence, and willpower."

"Yeah," I said, sometimes forgetting that Kira had once been an agent herself, "and then he spent the rest of the time throwing out different scenarios to see how I'd react." I raised my shoulders in a half-hearted shrug. "Not boring, but not all that exciting either."

"I remember those days," she mused. "Don't worry, you'll be learning how to disarm a bomb in no time." As my jaw went slack and my eyes widened, Kira erupted with laughter. "I'm kidding," she paused, "well, kind of. Just remember that when you're out in the field, anything can happen. All of the little exercises that they give to new recruits seem pointless at first, but when you're in a sticky situation, sometimes thinking back to the basics can actually help."

"Good to know," I drawled, pulling out a few older case files that Joe had given me to study. "What are you working on?"

"Just finishing up a new batch of healing solution," she said, grabbing a small beaker filled with a bright blue liquid after readjusting her safety glasses. Lifting the beaker to the larger distilling system she had set up, she slowly poured the liquid into the top, watching as it ran through the piping and landed in the clear solution at the bottom. "The infirmary's been running low for a while, so this needs to be mixed by the end of the day for it to have time to chill overnight."

"You have to freeze it?"

"Not entirely," she corrected. "Just enough for the molecules to vibrate slowly for a few hours and firmly mix together before we start storing it at room temperature."

I raised my eyebrows, an incredulous expression crossing my face. "Are you sure you weren't brought in as some kind of chemical genius?"

She shook her head. "One of the recruiters found me at women's homeless shelter about four years ago," she explained, her voice somber as she kept her eyes focused on the work she was doing. The fear and doubt was evident as she debated whether or not to continue. "My parents had kicked me out about a month before, and while out earlier that afternoon, I'd fought off a larger man who was looking for cash, having been trained in martial arts as a kid. At the time, I hadn't realized that S.I.C.O had already taken interest in me, and I didn't believe the recruiter when she first came to talk to me, but eventually I found myself here."

"Your parents kicked you out?" I asked in disbelief, not expecting my innocent question to cause our conversation to take such a serious turn.

A sad smile pulled at her lips as she nodded, her gaze lifting upwards to meet mine. "We had differing views on my sexual orientation."

The realization that she was a lesbian threw me for a moment, having not expected it, but what surprised me the most was that, just because of one insignificant detail, Kira's parents had had the audacity to shut her out of their lives. "Kira," I trailed off quietly, "I didn't know."

"It's not something I really talk about," she admitted, "plus, I gained a new family when I started training here, so I try not to dwell much on my past."

I searched for the right words to say – to let her know that if she did want to talk, I'd be there to listen, but before I could vocalize my thoughts, the familiar loud beep sounded throughout the room. We were no longer the only ones in the lab as Finn stepped inside, the grin on his face instantly brightening up the atmosphere.

"Ladies," he nodded in acknowledgement, making his way over towards a locked cabinet. "Kira, you mind if I grab some things for tonight?"

She shrugged. "You know the code," she replied, gesturing vaguely to the sheet that hung on the wall next to the cabinet, "just make sure to make a note of what you take."

He nodded in agreement, punching in a six-digit code before the metal door swung open, allowing him to reach inside and take what he needed. "So," he said, glancing towards me for a moment as he adjusted everything to fit into the belt around his waist, "what were you guys talking about before I barged in."

I looked towards Kira for a quick second to see a blank expression on her face, and it wasn't hard to infer that she wasn't keen to continue our conversation with Finn listening in. "Oh nothing," I replied after a short pause. "You know, girl talk."

Finn quirked an eyebrow as he cast his gaze between the two of us. It was clear he didn't believe the words that'd left my lips, but he didn't push, instead turning his back to us as he wrote down what he'd taken from the storage cabinet. "Have you spoken to your mom yet?" he asked as he locked up the cabinet, changing the subject entirely as he directed his question towards me.

I shook my head, stopping when I realized that, with his back turned, he couldn't see it. "No," I trailed, moving my fingers in a figure eight pattern on the surface of the table, "it's still weird to think of her like that."

Finn turned to face me, leaning back against the cabinet as he crossed his arms across his chest. "It was a pretty big shock to everyone, I think," he replied, "realizing that the Head of the Division had a child. We've all had time to digest it though; you haven't, so it makes sense that you're still adjusting."

"Every time someone mentions that she's my mom, I just keep thinking that my mom – the one I knew, died when I was eight," I admitted, the confession falling from my lips easily as I shrugged my shoulders. "I guess it's just going to take some time," I trailed, his words looping through my mind. "Hopefully in a few weeks I'll be able to talk to her about it."

I saw Kira nod as she finished off her work, but Finn simply shrugged his shoulders. "I mean, you can't really put a time limit on these things," he replied, walking towards me until he reached the other side of the table I sat at. "It took me a few months to get used to the idea."

"A few months?" I repeated with confusion, my eyebrows drawing together. "But Beckett said..." I trailed off, my eyes widening as I came to a sudden realization. "You were one of the agent watching out for me?"

His lips drew upwards lazily. "Guilty."

"So you knew who I was that first day in the cafeteria," I stated, and when he nodded in confirmation, I shook my head in disbelief. "Why didn't you tell me?"

He raised one shoulder, the smile not wavering from his lips. "Didn't think it was all that important."

"Sure it was," I replied, a light laugh escaping my mouth as I reached over and aimed a soft punch towards his shoulder, "I could've thanked you."

"I haven't seen you thank any of the other agents on your case. Even Beckett." Raising an eyebrow challengingly, I stayed quiet, smiling sheepishly because he was right. While I didn't know exactly which agents had been watching out for me, I certainly hadn't thought to thank Beckett. Instead, I'd had a constant feeling of anger and irritation towards him because he'd been the one to bring me here – that is, up until recently. "But I'll accept the thank you now if you're giving it, and I would say you're welcome, but it's kind of part of my job."

I rolled my eyes at his cheeky reply.

"But anyways," he trailed, pushing back from the table in a way that caused the arms of his t-shirt to tighten around his muscles, "I'd better get going. I have to meet up with my partner for tonight's assignment." He winked, his smile still gleaming. "More damsel's in distress to protect."

"I'll see you later," I said, shaking my head in amusement as I watched him leave, and when the door shut behind him, I turned to Kira. "Is he always that... that..."

"Happy?"

That was the simplest way to explain it, but failing to find another word, I nodded, letting a laugh escape. "Yeah."

"Ever since I met him," she affirmed, taking off her gloves and safety glasses. She moved to sit with me as she let the solution she had finished set. "But I know that he hasn't always had the easiest time."

"What do you mean?"

"I've never talked to him about it directly," she trailed, pausing for a short moment, "but it's pretty common knowledge that his parents both died while out on an assignment a while back." I felt a pull in my chest as the corners of my lips turned downwards. "When S.I.C.O agents have children, it's common for them to either be put up for adoption or be sent to live with another family member if the agents don't retire, but his parents were one of the few who tried to build a life outside of the Division."

A small part of me was conflicted, knowing that my mom wasn't the only one who put her child up for adoption, but the rest of me was more focused on listening to what Kira had to say.

"He doesn't talk about his past, but I think he was thirteen or fourteen when he was brought into the Division the night of his parent's funeral," she explained, "and from what I've heard, he started his training as one of the rare teenage agents relatively quickly. I'm pretty sure him and Beckett even trained together for a while, because at the time, they were the only ones young enough that still had to earn a high school diploma."

"Do you know why they don't get along then?" I asked, the question immediately falling into my head. Just knowing about both of their pasts, the similarities were evident, and while I could easily imagine the two of them becoming friends as they grew up together inside these walls, they seemed as though they could hardly stand the sight of one another. But I knew there was something more to it.

"You've noticed that too?" she mused.

"The sneers, the narrowed gazes, and the general avoidance? Yeah, I've noticed."

"Honestly," she continued, "I don't really think anyone knows exactly why they don't get along. I've been here for almost four years and I've never heard anybody bring it up. It's like it's taboo."

"Seriously?" I asked in astonishment, thinking that at least one person within the Division must know what went down between the two of them. Someone besides the men in question.

She nodded. "I couldn't tell you if something happened between them or if they just never got along, because I don't know," Kira explained, "but whatever it is, I'm guessing that's why they're complete opposites – one of them ice cold and the other burning with energy."

Even though I'd spent numerous hours with them both, and had come to accept that they had different ways of approaching the tasks they were given, I hadn't exactly realized how much their personalities clashed. Kira was right. Beckett liked to keep to himself – a strong and silent type, while Finn was fun-loving, outgoing, and appeared to get along with almost everyone.

When I didn't respond, stuck in my own thoughts, Kira shrugged her shoulders, her lips pulling upwards tepidly. "The longer you're here, the more you'll realize that everyone has some kind of story that they keep to themselves," she said, not only referring to Beckett and Finn, but to what she'd shared with me as well. "Whether it's something that they're holding onto from the life they lived before S.I.C.O– be it good or bad, or something that changed their perspective on the way their life is now, it's a way to stay grounded and stay true to yourself amongst the craziness."

Chapter 11

By the time the sun dropped below the treetops the following evening, I'd managed to build up a small amount of courage. Not enough to talk to Catherine, but certainly enough to make my way down to the training barn to find Beckett.

It wasn't extremely late, just past eight 'o'clock, meaning that the grounds were still quite lively with people squeezing in their evening training. People milled around the training barn specifically – almost too many people, and when I squeezed my way through the small crowd, it didn't take me long to realize why.

With my eyes wide, I watched as Finn and Beckett stood in the center of the room, their steps calculated as they sized each other up and prepared to fight. Before I knew it, Finn stepped forward and aimed a punch at Beckett's stomach, quickly following it up with another towards his jaw. Beckett's reflexes were sharp however, and he made the work it took to dodge the hits seem effortless. Quick to retaliate, Beckett shifted sideways before aiming a hit at Finn's upper body and a kick towards his ankles.

The back and forth went on for what seemed like forever – both fighters skilled in their movements as I stood at the forefront of the crowd, entranced with the fluidity of the moves and the underlying anger that each attack held. Realistically, by the time Beckett had finally managed to manipulate Finn's stance to his advantage, landing a particularly hard kick to his upper thigh and grabbing a hold of his arm to twist it behind him, only a few minutes had passed. Holding my breath as I watched Beckett tighten the hold he had on Finn, I didn't know whether I was routing for a win or hoping for Finn to escape.

Although it appeared to an untrained eye that Finn had no option other than to tap out and admit defeat, I hadn't noticed the slight movement in his feet as he inched his right backwards slowly before twisting his ankle around Beckett's. Finn sunk to the ground and slipped from Beckett's hold as he stepped backwards to regain his balance, and as Finn rose to two feet, he appeared confident with his fists clenched and ready to go, the last few moments pushed from his mind.

"Is that all you've got?" Finn asked, raising an eyebrow tauntingly as a smug grin appeared on his lips.

A fire ignited in Beckett's eyes as they narrowed and he clenched his jaw. Slanting his body away from Finn, he didn't attack right away, instead waiting with his arms lifted in a defensive position as he tracked the small movements of the man that stood across from him. When a small area on Finn's side appeared open, Beckett's reaction was immediate. He ducked into a squat as he threw the hit, hoping to avoid a counter shot, however, I doubt he expected Finn's elbow to lift out of position.

Landing a cheap shot on Beckett's jaw, Finn took advantage of having the upper hand by lifting his knee and slamming it hard into Beckett's chest before he could stop him. The only sound that could be heard as Beckett stood tall and took yet another hit from Finn was a small gasp, and only when the eyes of others momentarily turned my way, did I realize that it'd come from me.

As I watched Finn step back and Beckett regain a secure position, I pulled the corner of my bottom lip in between my teeth, feeling a rush of nerves flow through me as my eyes flitted between the two of them. I was waiting to see what the next move would be – waiting to see how this fight would end.

My eyes were drawn to Beckett as I noticed the slight shift in his position. I wasn't skilled enough to take a guess at what his attack would be – an uppercut punch, a roundhouse kick, or a combination of the two, but what I wasn't expecting was for him to take two steps back, lift his hands up in a surrender position, and bow his head in defeat.

The silence that had settled over the crowd was broken in an instant as everyone around me swarmed to the center of the training barn. What was just moments ago seen as a space to beware of was now a free for all. I was jostled from side to side as people pushed past where I stood, unmoving while I tried to follow the craziness. Both Finn and Beckett were stuck in the center of it all, but as they were approached by other agents, I noticed, and not for the first time, how different the two of them were.

I watched as Finn got swept up in the theatrics of it all; a wide smile on his face as he stood and happily accepted the congratulations and words that others offered. Beckett however, slowly tried to disappear into the shadows, moving backwards through the crowd and towards the edge, only acknowledging people with a quick nod of the head. When he stepped out of the crowd, his head ducked and his hands tucked inside his pockets, it was as if nobody noticed. He'd successfully diverted any attention that'd previously been on him, and as he slipped out of a small side exit, I took one last glance around the room to see that I was the only one who'd watched him go.

Retreating from the training barn, the darkness in the sky resembled that of thick black velvet, with only a few stars shimmering down and casting a soft glow on the grounds. It was enough to blur that which was far away, but luckily, I was still able to catch site of a figure moving quickly away from me, trying to remain unnoticed.

Beckett's steps began to slow once he rounded the edge of the main building and the training barn was no longer in view. He likely believed that he'd made his escape, but little did he know, his leisurely pace simply gave me the chance to catch up to him.

"So I guess training tonight is out of the question?" I asked, going for the direct approach as I made myself known.

I'd thought my appearance would at least startle him a bit, but as he turned to face me with his eyebrow quirked, the lack of surprise in his features cemented the fact that he known I'd been following him. "For now," Beckett replied shrugging his shoulders as he shifted his gaze back to the path in front of us. "I'll see if it quiets down later."

"And how would you feel about somebody joining you?"

"You?" he clarified, and I nodded as he stole a glance my way. "I guess that depends."

"Beckett," I started, his name the only word it took for his steps to halt and for him turn to face me. Straightening my posture and pushing my shoulders back, my voice was determined. "I understand what you said to me that night in the training barn – that I'm not in any position to be taking on anyone in the Gemini Clan." As much as I didn't want to admit it, I knew it was true. "But I do want to learn how to fight. I want to be able to protect myself – to protect others if the situation arises."

I didn't know what else I could say to convince him, and as he stood across from me, his eyes roaming over my features intently, the only thing that could be heard was the wind whistling around us.

His expression was void of any clues as to what he was thinking as he asked, "how come you're not asking Westin to help you?"

Having only heard Finn's last name a few times over the last month, it took me a moment to realize who he was talking about. "Because he beat you tonight?" He nodded, to which I shrugged my shoulders. "Finn's a friend," I said, "but even though you backed out of the fight tonight, I could tell you were the better fighter." A flash of emotion zoomed through his irises, and I could tell he was impressed by my response. "And out of curiosity, why did you back out?"

Finn's hits had been aggressive when he'd fought and were sure to leave bruises, but I knew just from watching Beckett fight in the past that he could've easily recovered and fought back.

"I don't particularly enjoy getting injured during training sessions," he replied, as though the answer to my question was obvious. "They're meant to hone your skills, challenge you to think outside the box, and strategize new attacks on different opponents. It just so happens that Finn and I get paired up every few months to train together."

"That didn't look like training," I pointed out, "it looked like something personal."

He reached a hand up to drag it through his hair, frustration emanating off him as he ground his teeth. "That happens whenever the two of us get paired together in the rotation," he explained, a rough edge to his words. "Everyone knows that we don't exactly get along, so when we're scheduled to train together, people find it entertaining to watch us fight."

"And I'm guessing that's not something you enjoy?"

"I don't care for the spectacle," he replied. "If Finn wants to bate me and throw in some dramatics to impress people, I'm not going to take it. It's not my style, so it's easier to just step out of the fight."

Talking to Beckett always seemed to be hit or miss. Replies either came quickly and the conversation flowed easily, or the atmosphere around us filled with thick tension that clouded my thoughts and made it difficult to know what to say. Tonight it appeared to be the former, which was why my next question slipped from my lips with ease.

"Can I ask why you and Finn don't get along?" I asked, casting a shot in the dark as I searched for clarity on what exactly had come between them.

A heavy sigh escaped him, and with no astonishment present in his features, I could tell that in some form or another, he'd expected my question. He pivoted on his heel, starting once again to follow the gravel path beneath our feet, and my footsteps fell alongside his.

"It's not some big thing," he revealed. "When he started here we were similar in age and we were both young. We had similar pasts, having both lost our parents to the career we were now training for, and at first, it wasn't hard to get along. We were stuck together so often that it was almost a given that we'd grow close, but because we were both quiet, we didn't really talk all that much."

I raised an eyebrow as he mentioned Finn being quiet; the complete opposite of how he was now, but although I found it hard to believe, I listened on.

"Finn caught up with the training pretty quickly, but the more he learned about S.I.C.O, it was like a switch flipped inside him. The more he knew, the more he wanted to find out. He began branching out and talking to the experienced agents, taking in any bits of information they'd give him, and suddenly he seemed like a stranger to me." He paused for a moment, letting the silence linger between us as I absorbed his words. "Like I said, it wasn't some big fight – we just didn't see eye to eye on some things as our training progressed, and now, I just don't fully trust him."

There was a part of me that'd been hoping for a juicier story than the one he'd given me. One that involved a fight, an assignment gone wrong, or something more than clashing views and differing opinions. My expression must've given my thoughts away, as I noticed the corner of his lip curl upwards.

"What? Expecting something more exciting?"

I shrugged, though he'd been spot on. "Kind of," I admitted, "but I'm also wondering why everyone makes such a big deal about it."

"People are strange," he replied. "Even more so considering almost everyone here has been trained to dissect actions and put a meaning to them."

"I guess there's just some things that we have no control over."

He nodded, and for a moment, it seemed like he wanted to say something more, though decided against it last minute as the silence surrounding us was broken. As we came up on a complete lap of the grounds, the voices from the training barn began to grow louder, and I knew that heading any further would be the last thing Beckett would want to do.

As I expected, his steps came to a slow stop as we reached the nearest entrance to the main building. "You know," he started, looking past me and out at the forest, "you always seem to be in the right place at the wrong time."

While it could be misconstrued as offensive, the careful way his words were spun, paired with the light tone of his voice led me to believe that he'd meant it to be a compliment – as weird as it sounded. "I do what I can."

The smallest and most discreet smile crept onto his lips, and if I were to blink, I would've missed it. "I'll see you tomorrow Aspen," he trailed as he stepped backwards and turned to move towards the main building. He looked back over his shoulder once before his body molded into that of a shadow in the darkness. "Meet me here for training when you're ready."

In a state that rested somewhere between sleep and awareness, a short, incessant beeping roused my senses. At first I felt annoyance seep through my body, grumbling under my breath as I tried to fight my way back to the peacefulness of my dreams, but the more alert I became, the louder the sounds grew.

As my eyes flew open, it took me less than a second to realize that something was wrong.

Sirens as loud as fireworks were going off through the entirety of the building, and as I pulled the covers off my body, throwing my legs over the side of my bed, a quick glance to the clock told me that it was still the middle of the night.

A commotion could be heard throughout the halls. Grabbing the sweater that I'd thrown to the foot of my bed earlier that evening, I slipped on a pair of shoes and was immediately thrust into the madness as I pulled open my bedroom door. Worried screams pierced through the crowd as younger trainees scrambled to follow the senior agents, but while they successfully masked their fears, it was clear by their rushed movements that they knew no more than anybody else.

Moving forward, I was immediately shoved to the side and jostled through a throng of people. Sheer panic clouded the air as the stone structure rumbled beneath our feet, and as I reached the staircase that led down to the main level, the urgency of the situation became stronger.

I had no idea what was happening, but as I listened closer to the blaring sirens, my eyes widened with fear.

Three consecutive alarms – which meant there'd been a security breach.

My composure was hanging by a thread and as I stumbled down the last few stairs, I only narrowly avoided bringing a group of others down with me as my hand reached out and grabbed the banister at the last minute. Righting myself, I was immediately pushed from behind and a sharp pain ignited at the base of my spine. I held myself together though, pushing forward before I hit the congestion that funneled towards the exits.

I didn't know what was happening or who had caused the breach – nobody did, and the uncertainty of the situation was what caused the frenzy of fear.

When I finally stepped out into the fresh air, a strong gust of wind attacked my hair, sending it flying in every direction, but I was able to breathe easier. I tried to get my thoughts in order as I moved further towards the forest – to bring a bit of organization to the chaos that surrounded me, but it was next to impossible as I also trained my gaze to scan the crowd for a familiar face.

"Aspen!"

Kira's voice tore through the air and as I turned my attention to the right, I saw her pushing her way past a group of people to get to me. She gripped her hand around my wrist as soon as she reached me, pulling me further away from everyone as people started to spread out.

"Kira," I said, pulling my arm free from her grip and placing my hands on her shoulders to stop her jitters, "what's going on?"

"I don't know," she said forcefully, though her voice was quiet enough that no one turned to look our way. "We haven't had a security breach in years."

My eyes widened at that intel. Although I was sure the building was constantly on high alert due to the classified activities that the Division partook in, I would've assumed a security breach wouldn't be all that rare. The fact that it'd been so long since the last one brought an unsettling feeling to my stomach as I wondered why, now that I was here, was everything going wrong.

The answer however, came with Kira's next words.

"The only people stupid enough to risk sneaking onto our grounds are the agents working for the Gemini Clan," she said with a certainty that couldn't be argued. A mixture of worry and relief glazed over her eyes when I inhaled sharply. "That's why I'm glad you're safe."

"You think they're here?" I asked shakily.

For some reason, the thought that the Gemini Clan were behind this attack had completely skipped my mind, but it made perfect sense. As far as I knew, they were the cause of most of the threats and problems Division 27 was dealing with, and while I didn't have much intel on current assignments, I wasn't naïve enough to think that whatever plan they were concocting had come to a halt just because I was out of their reach.

Or at least I thought I was.

"If they were," she trailed in response, "I doubt they stayed around long."

I felt a small panic ignite in my chest at not only the fact that there was a chance the Gemini Clan had infiltrated the Division's security, but the knowledge that they would've needed help. Help from the inside.

Looking around, I scanned the crowd as though it'd be easy to spot the traitor. As though they'd stick out like a sore thumb, but with only a few weeks of training, I knew better. If an agent from Division 27 had truly helped the Gemini Clan, they'd be smart enough to act just as worried as everyone else. They'd hide in plain sight. My gaze met several in return, but most of them were practically strangers to me, which made it hard to find an ounce of betrayal in their features.

My mind was jumbled with apprehensive thoughts, and it was only when I locked eyes with Beckett through the sea of people that I found myself releasing the pent-up air from my lungs. It didn't matter that the sky above cloaked us in a blanket of darkness because the lights from the building were enough to bring a dull light to all its surroundings, allowing me to see even the smallest of details. The way that relief filled Beckett's features as his purposeful steps came to a halt and the tension in his shoulders instantly dissipated.

The corner of his lips twitched upwards in a genuine smile and I felt my lips mirroring his movements, but it didn't last for long.

It seemed as though he was about to step forwards when his movements froze. His eyes hardened, his jaw clenched, and his muscles went rigid. Confusion fell over me for only a moment, because the next, I felt a pair of strong arms wind around my shoulders and pull me sideways.

I didn't need to pull back to know that it was Finn who had wrapped me up in a hug, and as if on instinct, my arms snaked up around his neck to fall into the comfort. The small break from reality as I closed my eyes and sunk into the embrace was exactly what I needed, but when I pulled back, I quickly turned to glance back at where Beckett had been just moments before. I bit my lip in concern as a tightness squeezed my heart when I noticed he was gone.

"Are you alright?" Finn asked, his voice filled with worry.

I brought my gaze back towards him and watched as his eyes scanned quickly over my features for any sign of injury. "I'm fine," I said reassuringly, taking another step backwards and crossing my arms over my chest. "It's just a bit of a shock, that's all."

"I'd say," he agreed, an unreadable expression crossing his face as his eyes flitted between Kira and I, "especially considering what some people are saying."

"You mean about the Gemini Clan," Kira interjected forcefully.

My forehead creased with confusion as I saw a silent conversation going on between the two of them. Finn's eyes widened marginally in response to Kira's narrowed expression – a small movement that I might not have noticed if my senses hadn't been on high alert.

"What?" I asked, knowing that I was clearly being left in the dark about something. "What am I missing?"

A grimace pulled at Kira's lips as Finn ducked his head and hunched his shoulders with guilt, avoiding my gaze at all cost. "Look around Aspen," Kira replied faintly.

Doing as she asked, I maneuvered my gaze over the chaotic crowd that surrounded me, not knowing exactly what I supposed to be looking for. I'd already scanned the crowd several times since the alarms sounded, noticing nothing more than the fear and confusion that'd been painted over everyone's facial expressions.

This time however, it was like I was looking at a different crowd. It became immediately apparent what Kira had wanted me to see – the way that everyone's eyes flickered towards me with a harshness that caused me to flinch.

"What – " I trailed, my voice shaking with bewilderment, " – is going on?"

Kira gulped. "There's been a lot going on with the Gemini Clan recently," she admitted, "and not just before you were attacked. Since you've been here it's like their actions have become more frequent. More of their attacks have been successful and we're no closer than before to figuring out exactly what they're planning."

"And with your mom's past coming back into the light, people are suspicious that it might not all be coincidental," Finn added carefully.

A pit of worry opened in my chest, however it was quickly overshadowed by the rush of anger that flooded my veins. I'd been left in the dark about all of this, and with the way I'd been steadfast with my mindset of avoiding Catherine, I'd heard none of the whispers that were clearly floating around. "What past?"

"After you were born," Finn started, "there were a lot of questions directed towards her character, her actions, and how well she truly fit in at S.I.C.O."

I felt the colour slip from my skin. I wanted to believe that what he was saying wasn't true – that he was lying, because pushing my personal feelings aside, I knew she was a good leader and a good agent. The people that worked with her and stood by her were a testament to that, but that was now. I had no idea what she'd gone through the last twenty-one years.

Anything was possible.

"There was a trial, for what I'm not really sure – that's seriously classified information around here," he explained, "but I do know that she was cleared of any allegations that were put against her. They transferred her over to Division 27 after everything was settled, and she's been here ever since."

"Then why do people think that all of this comes back to her? To me?" I asked as things failed to add up.

"Think about it," Kira said softly, stepping back into the conversation with caution. "Nobody knows exactly why Catherine was on trial all those years ago, but people have their guesses." My eyebrows drew together as I tried to think of a reason that would make sense and fit into the puzzle, but when I couldn't, Kira sighed. "There's speculation that she was linked to the Gemini Clan."

"Are you fucking kidding me?"

The words were out of my mouth quicker than my brain could process her statement. It couldn't be. There was no way that Catherine – who now stood as one of the leaders of the organization that wanted the Gemini Clan disbanded once and for all, had once been linked to them.

Glancing around, the sharp and accusing gazes had not only intensified, but they'd multiplied.

"Oh god," I inhaled, and it wasn't panic that reignited in my chest, but outrage at the situation. The speculation was absurd, as no one knew the whole story, but without the truth there was no way to put the rumours to rest.

Gritting my teeth and spinning on my heel, I ignored the calls from Kira and Finn as I pushed my way through the crowd. They wouldn't be able to change my mind. It didn't matter to me that it was the middle of the night or that we were in the middle of dealing with a security breach, because I needed answers.

And I wanted them now.

Chapter 12

My elbows were raised and my head ducked as I weaved my way through the sea of people while the alarms continued to cut through the air. I'd reduced the sounds to nothing more than background noise, directing my focus to the task at hand. As paranoia fell over the crowd however, the worried whispers were hard to ignore.

A series of chatter built up around me, all based upon the assumption that I was the enemy, and it sparked a fire in my chest. The urgency of the situation intensified, though as I reached the front of the crowd, I stopped dead in my tracks and stepped slowly backwards until I was once again hidden.

The doors I'd come out of were now lined with senior agents. They stood as guards to prevent us from returning to the building, and I knew there was no chance that I'd be able to convince them to let me pass, let alone have them let me go in on my own.

Which left me to find my own way inside.

I kept an eye on the agents as I moved, this time slower, trying not to draw any further attention to myself. The crowd, which seemed expansive as I trudged my way through the center, began to thin out as I circled the side of the building. Very few people had left the building through the east wing, as the housing quarters were found on the west side, and those who had were quick to join the other agents, not wanting to stand alone.

Hovering at the edge of the masses, I trained my gaze further along the building, and as I caught sight of a familiar gazebo in the distance, I remembered the door that led directly into the library. A hum of triumph coursed through me, knowing it was highly likely that, with the chaos that was ensuing, the side entrance had been overlooked.

Glancing over my shoulder twice for good measure, it was only when I was sure that I no longer stood as the object of people's concern that I made my move. I didn't run, but instead walked calmly, putting one foot in front of the other. The less I appeared to be acting out of the ordinary, the better off I was.

Once I was far enough away, I upped my speed, and just as a seed of optimism sprung to life at the sight of the unoccupied entrance, my steps staggered to a stop. Frozen, I watched as a shadow rounded the corner of the building, growing larger in the lights illuminating off the building. When I finally snapped out of my head, I jerked to the right, rounding the back of the gazebo and ducking swiftly out of sight.

My hands and knees dug harshly into the damp ground beneath me as I lifted my head to see two senior agents dressed for duty – wearing black cargo pants, tight black shirts, and their belts fully equipped. Having either been on night watch or recently returned from an assignment, their expressions were guarded and their footsteps heavy as they made their way around the building. When their eyes turned towards the gazebo, I dropped my head and laid horizontally across the grass, holding my breath and counting down the seconds until they averted their gaze, continuing their route around the building.

Staying in place as I exhaled slowly, I waited a few moments after the agents were out of sight to get to my feet.

My next movements were slow and calculated, because if I was already on people's radar as someone to watch out for, I didn't want to give them any other reason to question where my loyalties laid.

As I pulled the door to the library open, I stepped inside, laying my hands gently on the glass as I eased it closed behind me. When I heard the click of the latch, I felt a burst of relief flow from my muscles, but I knew I wasn't in the clear yet. The lights had been triggered in conjunction with the alarm, making it easy to find my way through the stacks, though I still made sure to stay light on my feet and hidden from view – just in case.

Stepping out into the hall, even the wariest of steps echoed against the stone. It was a drastic change from the scene outside, but somehow, I found the deserted corridors more intimidating than the suspicious crowd. If someone were to turn a corner, there'd be nowhere for me to hide, and just the thought caused my chest to tighten with an overpowering sense of anxiety.

But I couldn't back down.

I wasn't sure where Catherine would be in this state of panic. She may have very well been outside with the masses, but with a gut feeling leading my actions, I headed towards her office. It'd been a place I'd only visited once, my first day here, though over the last few weeks I'd seemed to have unknowingly memorized the route, making sure to avoid it at all costs.

Reaching the spiral staircase, I lifted my foot, and just as the bottom of my shoe hit the step, my breath caught in my throat as the alarms ceased overhead. Along with the sudden silence, every light in the vicinity abruptly flickered off, leaving me beneath a cloak of darkness.

My heart beat out of tune, shifting to a rapid staccato as I ascended the stairs. With my arms extended to the sides, my palms pressing lightly against the walls to guide me, it was only when I was steps away from the landing that I noticed the glare of light coming from the end of the small hallway.

And it was coming from Catherine's office.

Closing my eyes for a moment, I stayed put, forcing any thoughts of backing down out of my head as I reminded myself of the bigger picture. Catherine was hiding something – something important, and I was going to get the truth out of her, one way or another.

With my resolve hardened, I climbed the last of the stairs and saw that the door to her office was wide open. My hands clenched at my sides as I saw the silhouette of her shadow against the far wall, but I didn't make it another step.

A man's voice – deep and assertive, broke the silence. "You know that if you keep this up your agents will fall – one by one," he spoke, confident in his words, "and all you're doing is speeding up their demise."

It felt like a black hole had opened within my chest, sucking every organ and feeling towards the center.

Had people's assumptions been right? Had my mother been linked to the Gemini Clan all those years ago?

Worse yet, was she still?

It should have been fear that erupted inside of me, knowing that Catherine could've possibly been part of the plan to orchestrate my attack just so that she'd be able to watch over me, but instead it was anger. My blood boiled and my fists shook as something snapped within me.

I marched towards her office, each step heavy and filled with purpose, but as I reached the entryway, the scene before me caused the colour to drain from my skin.

Standing behind her desk, Catherine held a pistol between her hands, her arms extended straight in front of her as she pointed the barrel towards a man on the other side of her office. Her eyes were narrowed in a menacing gaze, and I could clearly see the veins in her neck pulsing as she clenched her teeth. "You need to leave, now," she said firmly, the underlying threat evident as the man across from her curled his lips upwards in a sickening grin.

"Now why would I want to do that?" he replied tauntingly, as though the gun pointed in his direction was nothing more than a piece of plastic. "You know why I came here tonight."

Up until then, I'd gone undetected – both Catherine and the man too focused on each other, but when a sudden, muffled whimper of fear slipped through my lips as I inched myself backwards, both gazes spun swiftly towards me.

"Aspen," Catherine gasped, her irises flashing with terror momentarily before she reestablished her guard.

"Well, well," the man drawled, a wicked gleam filling his features, "it looks like tonight's operation was worth it." He paused, his lips stretching wider at the fact that I cowered backwards another step. "It's good to finally meet you Aspen."

"Who are you?" I stuttered, my fingernails digging into my palms – deep enough to draw blood. "How do you know who I am?"

"Aspen," Catherine said sternly, her gaze now firmly on the man as she shifted her finger onto the trigger, "get out of here."

The laugh that passed through the man's lips was deep and malevolent, growing louder as it echoed off the walls. "Now Catherine, I'm sure she's waited a long time to be reunited with her parents," he said, "why deny her the chance?"

His words were a painful punch to the stomach, the air leaving my lungs in one fell swoop, causing me to stagger backwards. My eyes widened and I threw my arm out to the side, resting my palm against the wall to regain my balance. My gaze flitted towards Catherine, willing her to deny the accusation, but as the silence dragged on, her lips twisted painfully, cementing the words to be true.

"No." I shook my head in denial. "No, you're lying."

When he moved to step towards me, the sickening sound of a gunshot lit up the air. A high-pitched scream followed as I brought my left hand up to cover my open mouth in disbelief, my eyes trained on the bullet that had sunk into the wall not even three feet away from me.

Catherine had fired as a warning, but with the blazing heat that lit up her gaze, it was clear that the next bullet would be aimed at a different target.

"Leave now Damon," she said, her voice deadly.

My whole body tensed as he walked towards me, but seeing as I blocked the only visible exit, there was no way around it, much to my dismay. "I'm sure I'll see you again soon," he spoke, his words a whisper against the side of my face as he strolled past me, leaving nothing behind but the ghost of his presence.

Catherine slowly lowered the gun in her hands, clicking the safety back into place as she tucked it into the holster that rested on his hip. "Aspen – "

I cut off her plea, squeezing my eyes shut. "It's true, isn't it – " I swallowed, the words leaving a bad taste in my mouth. " – what he said? He's my father?"

When she failed to respond, I opened my eyes, watching as she met my gaze squarely and nodded her head grimly.

The confirmation was the final nail in the coffin for tonight, shattering the façade I'd built up. In the dark recesses of my mind, I knew that there was more to the picture than just the black and white facts, but in that moment, I couldn't conjure up a scenario in which anything made sense. "I'm sorry," I choked out, a plethora of emotions rolling over me at once, "I can't do this right now."

I was fast learning that I was incapable of facing any aspect of my past dead on, and just like when she'd told me the truth about being her daughter, I turned away from her. This time however, she didn't call out to try and stop me, because it was clear there was nothing she could do or say to make this better.

Returning to my room that night, I had the remnants of tears staining my cheeks, as well as an overworked mind as my head hit the pillow. I tossed and turned, willing myself to forget the last hour had ever happened, but it was no use. When the sun began its ascent into the sky, I was still awake, listening to the shuffling feet and quiet chatter outside grow.

Unable to muster the energy to lift myself from bed, I made use of the fact that my mind refused to relax and tried to sift through all that I knew.

Catherine and the man who'd infiltrated the Division last night – Damon, my mother had called him – were my parents. Watching the two of them stand on either side of a gun had been terrifying, but it also made me wonder exactly what had happened between the two of them in the first place. Had my dad been a mistake my mother had made, or was it once love that the two of them had shared?

Either way, it was clear that there was now a divide between them, and the one conclusion my mind immediately jumped to was that Damon, whoever he may be, was a part of the Gemini Clan.

It made sense – why she would've given me up as a baby, why she'd supposedly been put on trial all those years ago, and why she'd held him up at gunpoint.

Rolling over in bed, I heaved in a deep sigh as frustration and anger coursed through me, and with my face dug deep into my pillow, I screamed. It was the only release I could think of, and as the thick material absorbed the high-pitch sound, I could feel the dissipation of stress from my body.

It wasn't much, but it was something.

Only hours later did I leave my room, when my stomach craved something of sustenance and I had successfully lazed around for as long as I could. I'd reorganized the few things I had, gone through a few notes I'd taken while learning French, and simply watched from my window as other agents walked the grounds – moving in small groups with worry flooding their features.

The paranoia grew larger as I walked the halls, succumbing to the scrutinizing looks and conversations that dropped to hushed whispers as I passed by. After last night, it seemed that everyone was out of the loop – all wanting to know who had set off the security alarms, but even though my thoughts were conflicted, I stayed tight lipped.

I had no idea if Damon had managed to get away unseen, or if he'd been alone, and it wasn't something I wanted to be thinking about.

Keeping my head ducked, I avoided making eye contact with other agents as I made my way towards the Grand Hall. Even as I joined the short line for food, I could feel the piercing stares hitting my back, and they didn't waver as I moved through the room towards the back. Facing the wall as I found a seat away from the crowd, I willed the phrase out of sight, out of mind to do wonders, tapping my fingers rhythmically atop the table as I ate.

It was only when I was nearly finished that I heard foot-steps approaching, causing my shoulders to tense and my arm to freeze in mid-air, only to exhale and relax as I stiffly turned my head to see Kira heading towards me.

"Aspen," she sighed gratefully, "there you are. I've been looking everywhere for you."

I quirked an eyebrow. "And you didn't think to check here?"

"It's not exactly lunch time," she pointed out – which was true, seeing as it was just after two in the afternoon, "and I figured you'd be hiding in your room or holed up somewhere quiet after last night."

I could hear the pity that seeped into her words as she trailed off, though I didn't let it show. After I'd stomped off, abandoning both her and Finn in the crowd, she had no idea that I'd made my way back into the building and up to my mother's office before the sirens had been cut off. To the best of her knowledge, I'd let anger overtake my actions and had had to walk away, and though an unnerving feeling rushed through me as I withhold the truth from her, I knew that I had to. At least for the time being.

"You must've just missed me then," I replied breezily, "I came down about twenty minutes ago."

She nodded in understanding, taking a quick glance at my tray. "Joe asked me to find you," she explained. "He said he had something he wanted to work through with you before the end of the day."

"I'm free now," I said, twisting as I stood from the bench and grabbed my empty tray, "I just figured he'd be busy today."

She shook her head. "Catherine and a few of the top agents are working to figure out the logistics of everything that went down last night – who was involved, how they got through our security, and what exactly they wanted."

I didn't know what was worse – knowing the truth (at least a part of it) and having to keep quiet, or not knowing a thing and letting the unknown haunt your thoughts.

"Joe hasn't been all that involved though, as far as I know," Kira continued as the two of us left the Grand Hall and headed for the room he always had on reserve for our training sessions. It didn't take long, and as we approached the open door, I saw Joe standing alone. His head was down, his attention being taken by the phone in his hands, though as he glanced up and saw the two of us, he hurriedly tucked the phone into his back pocket.

"There you are," he said, his lips pulling upwards as he waved the pair of us in. "When I told Kira to fetch you, I didn't expect you'd be back so fast."

From the mess spread out across two of the tables, I took that to mean that he wasn't done setting up whatever he had planned. There was a mass of thin wires tangled up across the surface, all hooked up to an old-style looking laptop, but what threw me off was the arm band and loose wires that added to the pile.

"What is all this?" I asked as I stepped further into the room, running my hands over the machine before looking back to Joe for an answer.

"It's a lie detector," he replied, moving around the table to unravel the mess. "As an agent, it's important to be able to keep calm and stick to the plan, even in extremely stressful or life-threatening situations. I figured, after everything that went down last night, today would be a good day to hook you up and see how well you can do keeping to a story I've prepared. All you'll have to do is answer the questions accordingly and trust your instincts. But also, remember that this machine picks up the changes in your heartbeat and spikes in blood pressure, so you'll have to remain calm throughout the entire situation."

Impressed by the machine, and intrigued at what he had in store for me, I agreed, taking a seat in one of the chairs. Kira helped Joe with the set up – starting up the program on the computer and tightening the wires that had to be attached to my body. When all was said and done, I had an arm band squeezing tightly around my bicep, three nodes attached to different sections of my head, two nodes resting at the base of my spine, and three of my fingers wrapped in node rings, the wires all running back to a small box that was attached to the laptop.

Kira was just finishing the readjustment of the nodes on my back when I heard the click of metal and felt a heavy weight fall around my ankle.

Looking down, my heart beat sporadically in my chest as I saw that my left foot had been shackled to the base of the chair, and before I could do anything else, I felt a belt slide across my stomach, locking me down.

"What the hell?" I exclaimed, my eyes wide as I looked between Kira and Joe, trying and failing to shake myself free of the holds. "What the fuck is going on?'

There was regret in Kira's eyes as she stepped away from me, but that only cemented that this had been part of the plan all along. "I'm sorry," she spoke, her voice filled her emotion, "but this is for your own good. I saw you last night... and you can't let your emotions control you like that in the field – there's too much at stake."

I could see the tears forming in her eyes, her words accompanied with an undertone that could only come from experience, but that didn't matter. What mattered was that she'd been an accomplice in locking me down and making me immobile, and I didn't know if this was part of the drill, or if this was something much, much worse.

When I opened my mouth to ask what she was talking about, all that came out was a strangled groan as Catherine walked through the door.

"You did this?" I hissed moments later, glaring at Kira as she moved backwards, heading for the door.

"Yes, and when this is over, I hope you remember what a waste it is to push away the people trying to help you," she replied, her voice quiet but her words firm, causing a dagger to spear my chest in a way to painful to describe.

Clenching my eyes shut, I could feel my heart pounding furiously and could hear the roar of blood in my ears, but not another word was said as she left the room, closing the door on her betrayal.

Chapter 13

I could feel my breathing getting shallower as panic set in.

"Aspen," Catherine said worriedly, watching my features shift as she slowly moved towards me, "this isn't what you think."

"Isn't – isn't what I think?" I stuttered, inhaling sharply as I tried to pull the reins on my emotions. I narrowed my eyes and clenched my jaw, struggling against the restraints that held me in place. "What am I supposed to think right now?" I asked incredulously, my voice growing louder with each word. "Everyone here thinks that I had something to do with the alarm last night, all because I'm related to you, and considering it was my father who somehow broke into the Division unseen, I'm starting to think that maybe they aren't wrong for having trust issues. After all, someone had to help him get inside."

By the way that Joe's skin paled and his eyes widened, it was clear that Catherine hadn't told him the truth about what'd gone down last night. "Damon was here?" he asked in disbelief, his gaze shifting towards Catherine.

And even though I expected her to be angry that I'd let that bit of information slip – to narrow her eyes or vehemently deny the accusations, she didn't.

Instead, she looked defeated.

"He was," she admitted weakly, her gaze on the ground and her shoulders hunched.

His gaze became murderous as he stepped closer to her. "And you saw him?"

Though she didn't flinch at the force behind his words, she swallowed thickly, nodding as she debated what to tell him. "He knew that once the alarms were activated everyone would be scrambling," she admitted, though I wasn't sure if what she was saying was true. After all, agents, especially skilled ones, were trained in the art of deception. "He also knew that I'd go to my office to oversee the grounds and act as the front line of defense within the building, because when I got there, he was already there."

"How did he even get in?"

By this point, it was as if Joe had forgotten I was there. His back was facing me and his focus was solely directed towards my mother as I sat silently, watching the interaction and soaking in any useful information.

"I don't know how he got onto the grounds unnoticed, but the timing doesn't add up. To get to my office that quickly, he would've had to scale the building, and while it's a possibility, I think he had help. Either he wasn't acting alone or – "

" – he had help from one of our own," Joe finished for her, to which she nodded solemnly.

The silence stretched on as they both considered the possibility that someone within Division 27 had helped Damon, but after a few moments, Joe was the one to break it. "What did he want?" he asked, and although it was an automatic reaction to the question, he immediately trailed his eyes over her in search of any wounds or bruises.

There was a flash of intensity in her eyes that faded as quickly as it'd appeared, and while I couldn't grasp what it meant, that didn't stop Joe's eyes from widening in understanding.

"Look," I interrupted, bringing their attention back to me as I rattled the chains that secured me to the chair, "I don't think you brought me here just to listen to the two of you discuss something that's clearly private, so for the love of god, just let me go."

Catherine's resolve toughened at my words as she looked to Joe.

"No," he said firmly, turning to face me before he stepped forwards to adjust the lie detector. "I brought you here because this," he gestured between Catherine and I, "has gone on for far too long. Now, neither of you can change what's been said and done in the past, but that doesn't mean you can't move past this."

"But – "

Joe held his hand up to stop me. "But nothing." I grinded my teeth together in frustration as I watched him untangle the remaining wires for the lie detector, but this time, instead of placing them on me, he motioned Catherine over and began to hook her up. "Your friends are worried about you Aspen, and frankly, I am too. Emotions are a part of us – they're what make us human, but when you let them affect the way you act and the way you think, especially in the field, they can be dangerous. You need to be able to trust the agents that stand by your side."

"How am I supposed to trust someone who seems hell-bent on keeping things from me?" I asked snidely.

"That's why we're here," Joe explained, pressing a button on the laptop so that the program started, a steady buzzing coming from the speakers as a flat green line ran across the screen. "Both of you will be hooked up to the lie detector – you, Aspen, so that you'll be able to see that it works, and her," he pointed to Catherine as he addressed me, "so you can get the answers you want and clear the air between the two of you."

I quirked an eyebrow in disbelief. "And you agreed to this?" I asked, glancing towards Catherine suspiciously.

She nodded. "I did," she replied, and when I glanced towards the machine, the line stayed level.

I sat back disgruntledly in the chair, still aware of the fact that I was unable to move. I wanted to believe that they were telling the truth, that this my chance to get answers, but with so many holes left in the puzzle, I didn't know what to believe.

I'd learned a long time ago that when something seemed too good to be true, it normally was.

"Okay," Joe said, getting settled in a chair across from me when I didn't question them further. "Now let's start off easy, what's your full-name?"

I stared at him for a moment before I responded. "Aspen Rigby."

The line on the screen didn't waver, prompting Joe to continue. "And how are you dealing with everything that's happened over the last couple of weeks."

"Just fine," I replied, giving nothing away in my expression. When the line began to climb high and dip low in rapid succession, Joe's features tightened. I shrugged. "If either of you would've believed that without the machine telling you otherwise, you need to brush up on your skills."

"Next question then," Joe said, brushing off my words as if they were nothing. "Why did you want to start training to become an agent?"

"I didn't really have a choice, now did I?"

"You did," he countered, "and you made the choice to get involved."

I toyed with my thoughts for a moment, debating on which answer to give. While I hadn't had any doubts about the lie detector's skills to begin with, it seemed to be working, but if they felt the need to convince me, it didn't matter whether I chose to lie or tell the truth.

"Because I wanted to protect myself," I ended up saying truthfully. "In the beginning, I didn't care much about helping the Division in any way, shape, or form. I just wanted to make sure that if I was attacked again, like I was that first night, I'd have a better chance."

"And now?"

"Now," I trailed, hardening my gaze, "I think it's about time for me to be able to ask the questions."

What I failed to say was that I was now emotionally, physically, and mentally invested in S.I.C.O, and even though the Gemini Clan were seemingly after me, I knew that I was only a small part of their plan.

And I intended to find out what the bigger plan was.

Joe nodded in agreeance, motioning me to ask away, though I simply quirked an eyebrow at him and shook my leg – which was still chained to the chair. "I think I'd be able to concentrate more if I didn't feel like a prisoner wearing these shackles," I drawled.

The hesitation that crossed his face was immediate, and I had to stop myself from rolling my eyes. What did he think was going to happen?

"Let her go."

I concealed my surprised at Catherine's words, turning to see that while her features were impassive, her gaze was stuck firmly on me. Joe didn't question her however, despite his own wariness. Pulling a key from his pocket, he stepped forward, watching me carefully as he unlocked both my ankle restraint and the belt that wrapped tightly around my mid-section.

I could've leapt up from my chair in that moment and attempted a rush towards the door, but I knew it wouldn't have done me any good.

Besides, even though their approach was uncharacteristic, they were giving me a chance to settle the questions and concerns circling my mind, and I wasn't about to waste the opportunity.

Shaking out the ankle that'd been shackled, I took a few seconds to gather my thoughts before turning back to face her.

"Who is Damon?" I asked, cutting straight to the point, though before she could respond I continued. "And I don't want to hear some half-assed answer about him being my father. I want the full truth."

"He's a lying, manipulative son-of-a-bitch," she started without hesitation. "He's ruthless and he's conniving, and there's no doubt in my mind that he can twist the truth to convince those who fear him to do his bidding for him. And yes, he is your biological father, but as it stands right now, he's the sole leader of the Gemini Clan."

I gulped as she confirmed what I'd only guessed thus far; the lie detector staying level and undisturbed by her words.

"What happened then?" I asked, shaking my head as I trailed off. "How did you go from trusting him all those years ago to threatening to kill him more than twenty years later?"

"I was young and naïve," she admitted. The emotion in her eyes was evident as she struggled to keep herself together. We were behind closed doors, and with nobody to judge her, she was allowing her toughened exterior to fall. "I met him while on a mission and at the time I didn't know who he was. He didn't tell me about training as an agent or who he really was – he made up a completely new persona, and it was one that I slowly fell in love with."

"It was only when I caught him in a lie a year later that I grew curious and suspicious." There was a hitch in her breath before she exhaled slowly. "I found out he'd known exactly who I was the day he met me. Everything was a lie. He'd wanted to grow close to someone on the inside so that he'd have an alibi if things ever went downhill with his plans. By the time I broke it off with him and came clean to the Head of the Division I was working for at the time, he'd disappeared without a trace."

It was clear that Joe had heard this story before, as none of what Catherine had said seemed to surprise him. He stayed quiet as he sat next to her, though his expression pulled tightly with anger every time Damon was mentioned.

"And yesterday? Why didn't you call for back up?" I asked, pushing back the sympathy that began to settle in my chest as I thought logically. "You're supposed to be the one heading up the investigation to bring down the Gemini Clan, yet you hesitated when it mattered the most."

My gaze was drawn to the computer screen as the lie detector spiked slightly, and instead of being the result of a lie, it was due to the change in questioning. Her nerves were growing, and attached to the machine it was impossible to hide.

"If you're looking for a valid answer, I don't have one," she trailed, her voice losing conviction as her gaze dropped to the table. "At first I wanted to pull information out of him, knowing that I could use what I knew of him in the past to exploit him, but once you showed up, my only focus was keeping you safe."

"I heard him say that it didn't matter who died – he'd make sure to get what he wanted," I said, pausing as I flicked my eyes between her and Joe. "What is it that the Gemini Clan is after?"

Catherine didn't answer right away, instead taking a few moments as she debated what to tell me. "When S.I.C.O was first created over 150 years ago, the founders were skilled weapon crafters and ahead of their time with scientific advances," she explained. "They were trained to work deep undercover, collect intel from all reputable sources, and bring any usual information back to their labs for research. But one of their first trainees began to veer off track. He kept a low profile, but he saw things differently than everyone else – he saw how S.I.C.O's resources could be used for evil instead of good."

"When he was caught and sentenced to death, the foundation of the Gemini Clan had already formed, with other operatives working secretly on the inside. It took the founder's a long time to figure this out, but once the knowledge was out in the open, they started to tighten security. All their research went into lock down and their specially crafted weapons were hidden and replaced with new-age guns. As the years went on – with S.I.C.O growing larger and the Gemini Clan splitting off and going into hiding, the weapons became a mythic tale. One that some agents never quite let go of."

"And these weapons," I started, quirking an eyebrow, "S.I.C.O still has them locked up?"

Catherine nodded. "They're scattered around the globe, with only a few people truly knowing their location."

Her small evasions were enough to flip a switch in my mind. "One of them is here," I said, my eyes widening with realization, "isn't it?"

It would've been simple to deny it, but it was evident from the way she hesitated that I was on the right track. "Aspen – " she started carefully, as though she wanted to tell me the truth, but knew she couldn't.

"Look," I cut her off, "I don't need to know where it is, or even what it is. I just want to know how I fit into all of this, considering I didn't even know S.I.C.O existed until that first attack."

Catherine avoided looking me straight in the eye as her gaze moved to Joe – the two of them having a silent conversation. I noticed the way her features shifted. The way her jaw clenched and her lips thinned, but the longer I was left without a reply, the easier it was to read the signs and figure out the words they didn't want to say.

And the realization felt like a knife to the chest.

"Damon thought he could use my life as a bargaining chip to get what he wanted," I stated, my voice filled with dread.

"Yes," she responded bluntly.

My hands began to tremble as I looked towards the screen, hoping that the lie detector would spike and let me know that I'd been wrong – that her confirmation was a lie, but as the line stayed calm, my stomach rolled with fear.

I released a shaky breath as I gently pulled at the cords still attached to me. "I think that's enough," I said weakly, and neither of them stopped me as I stood up. I looked towards Catherine. "And I hope you know that this doesn't mean that

I forgive you, or that I suddenly trust you. I still want Joe to train me, but thank you, for telling me the truth now."

"You know you can't mention this to anyone – the weapons, Damon, any of it," Joe said, sounding as though he was speaking for Catherine.

I nodded as I moved around them and headed towards the door. "I know," I replied, "and don't worry, I won't."

Chapter 14

S eeing as it was mid-day, the halls were fairly empty. Everyone was likely out on assignment or throwing themselves into training – the paranoia and questions about the intrusion presumably still at the forefront of their minds. If Catherine continued to withhold the true reason for the alarm, there would no doubt be a stream of whispers throughout the halls in no time. People would draw their own conclusions based on farfetched assumptions, and knowing what I did, it almost seemed easier to be kept in the dark and tasked with the guess work.

With my mind whirling, I kept my head down and my steps purposeful as I made my way towards my room. It was the only place I felt like I could process what I'd learned without my thoughts and emotions going awry.

Shutting the door behind me minutes later, I let out a shaky breath.

No matter how small it'd been, there'd still been a part of me that had hoped my involvement in all of this was a fluke. That, despite the fact I was Catherine's daughter, the Gemini Clan had pulled my name up by accident. Now though, that hope was squashed. Damon, the leader of the Gemini Clan, was my father. He had intended to use me to bargain with S.I.C.O to obtain one of their original weapons.

The words, the facts, they replayed over and over again in my head, growing larger and more prominent with each second that passed. The rational part of my mind was telling me that Catherine had been sincere with her words – that her words had been true, but then there was the part of me that wanted to stay angry. And not just at the situation, but at everyone who'd been a part of bringing me to Division 27 in the first place. From Beckett to Catherine, Joe to Finn, all the agents that'd been assigned to protect me, and Kira, who'd betrayed my trust – all of them now stood as reasons why I couldn't go back to my old life.

Most of all however, my anger was directed towards the Gemini Clan. More specifically, towards their leader.

If Damon had never found out about me, I wouldn't be in this position. I wouldn't be learning to fight or going through training. I'd still be spending my days as a waitress at Crimson Oaks, saving up every penny so that I could build a future for myself. A future where I wouldn't have to think about the fact that my biological father had seen nothing wrong with the idea of using me as a bartering chip to get what he wanted.

Attempting to control myself as I felt anger pulsing through me, I stepped up to the window that overlooked the grounds. Though the sun was shining, there was no ignoring the strong gusts of wind that whistled against the glass, casting a parallel from the chaos inside my head. It was harsh, causing the trees to do a powerful dance as the leaves hung onto the branches for dear life. Their movement was what I focused on to calm my breathing, as crazy as it seemed, but the constant back and forth motion was rhythmic in a peculiar way.

The time passed quickly, and before long I could hear a slew of footsteps passing by my room. As I moved to sit at the top of my bed, each set of footsteps caused a rush of tension to flow through my veins, my thoughts momentarily put on hold as I worried that someone would knock on my door.

I didn't have the strength to deal with questions, much less the desire to hold a conversation with someone, and as the minutes ticked by and my door was left well enough alone, I began to slowly allow my body to relax into the comfort my bed offered. With the stress of the previous night hovering over my head, as well as the eventful day, I couldn't be bothered to leave the room to eat. My mind was shutting down, and just as the sun began to descend behind the trees outside, my eyes fluttered shut.

Occasionally throughout the night I jerked awake – my dreams a compilation of circumstances that would've had the ability to come to fruition if the attack against me on my birthday had been successful. The images that flashed through my head made for a less than peaceful night. Each time I awoke, I wavered in a state between awareness and slumber, and with exhaustion pumping through me, I had no willpower to fight against it before I fell back asleep.

That was, until I was startled awake for the fifth time. The morning was on the horizon, and as the sun rays cast a harsh glare through the window and into the room, I sighed, knowing it wouldn't do much good to try and fall back asleep for another time.

Forcing myself up and out of the bed, I headed into the bathroom. After jumping in the shower and rinsing off the remaining layer of sweat that had sheened to my skin, I pulled on a fresh set of clothes, hoping that today would be a better day.

It was early, and as my stomach growled with hunger, I knew there was no way to avoid the crowd of early risers. I could hear the footsteps of a handful of people coming back from overnight assignments or getting started with their day, and as I stepped into the hallway, I knew I was consciously leaving the sanctuary of my room behind.

I found myself holding my breath every time I turned a corner, hoping that I wouldn't run into anyone I was trying to avoid. Luck seemed to be on my side as I entered the Grand Hall to see no one I immediately recognized before making my way towards the food counter.

As my worries began to subside and I allowed my mind to relax, I piled my tray with a bowl of oatmeal, a few pieces of toast, and a much-needed cup of coffee. Just as I turned to find a spot to sit however, I was cut off when someone stepped in my path.

"Aspen."

My shoulders tensed at Kira's voice, though with no desire to deal with her in that moment, my grip on my tray tightened as I stepped swiftly to the side, trying to push passed her. It was no use however, as she reached out to grab my arm lightly, attempting to keep my attention.

"Aspen, please – "

I turned my head sideways to meet her pleading gaze. "Look, I seriously don't want to listen to what you have to say right now," I said, pulling my arm from her grip and continuing to walk away from her.

Though I didn't make it far.

Before my gaze had completely returned forward, I was stopped yet again as I bumped into someone, teetering slightly and flinching backwards as a stream of hot liquid seeped into my clothing. I was able to regain my balance, but as I looked down at the tray in my hands with wide eyes, I saw that it was my own drink that had emptied onto me.

I felt my eyes tighten as they narrowed, glancing upwards to see Beckett standing in front of me – a mixture of surprise and anger filling his features. The surprise I understood, but the anger, that was reserved for me.

"Are you fucking kidding me?" I seethed through clenched teeth.

His features tightened as he quirked an eyebrow. "If you think you can afford to blow off a training session," he started, his voice low enough so only Kira and I could hear, "you might want to work on paying attention to your surroundings."

It hadn't even crossed my mind the previous night that I'd stood him up for a training session he'd graciously offered. With everything that had happened in the forty-eight hours since, it'd been overshadowed.

My mistake was also far from my mind as my anger got away from me. Without much thought, I dropped my tray onto the counter closest to me, picked up my bowl of oatmeal, and raised it up before dumping the contents over Beckett's head.

The lines of anger in his features disappeared momentarily, replaced with bafflement and shock, though they reappeared after a few seconds had passed. His eyes narrowed and I noticed his jaw tick with annoyance.

"What was that for?" he asked roughly.

I didn't have an answer for him. I'd done it because, in the moment, it made me feel better to have an outlet for the emotions boiling inside of me. I didn't consider the fact that we stood at the front of the Grand Hall, and that, in response to our commotion, everyone's gazes turned our way.

The clinking of cutlery ceased, and before I could grasp onto what was happening, I felt a sticky substance splatter against my arm as an all-out food fight ensued around me. The room of professional agents – whether they were trainees or veterans to this Division, all seemed to lose their sense of inhibition after watching Beckett and I go at it.

Bacon, eggs, waffles, fruit – all of it, and more, went flying across the room, and in a rush to try and get out of the room unscathed, several agents fled from the Hall, bumping into me as they went. I was too shocked to do anything but watch the chaotic spectacle around me with wide eyes.

"Enough!"

Beckett's voice cut through the crowd sharply, and while the ceasefire was immediate, a group of younger agents – who didn't look much older than eighteen – looked to him with smug looks on their faces.

"Why start something you don't intend on finishing?" one of them asked, quirking an eyebrow challengingly.

"I would also like to know the answer to that," Catherine said, her voice echoing off the walls as she stepped into the room.

My posture stiffened as I – still standing next to Beckett – made eye contact with her as she waited for an answer. Any amusement and mirth that remained in the room was quickly shaken away as the silence dragged on. Catherine's gaze shifted as she scanned over the rest of the agents in the room. "I advise you all to head off and start your training for today, that is, if you don't want to be stuck cleaning up this mess."

I knew there was no sense in trying to slip out undetected, as she'd already pinned both Beckett and I as the ones responsible, but the message seemed to sink in for most others. There was a scramble as the Grand Hall emptied, and within a few moments, the only ones left standing alongside the food-stained tables were Kira, Beckett, and I.

"Ms. St. James," Catherine said, regarding Kira, "I suggest you head to the lab, unless you'd like to share the blame for this mess."

I didn't turn around to watch the emotions flash over Kira's features, but I heard a low sigh leave her lips before she moved passed me, her gaze dropped as she headed for the door.

"Now, you two, follow me."

Catherine said nothing more before turning on her heel and walking away. Beckett wasted no time in following her orders, though seemingly begrudgingly, while I stayed back a moment. Gulping down my fears and anger, I put one foot in front of the other, catching up with Beckett and falling into stride with him.

"This is all your fault," I muttered under my breath, just loud enough for him to hear me.

"Not likely."

His words were rough, and as we followed Catherine through the halls and towards her office, nothing more was said. Instead, the anticipation over what would happen began to grow. How would she react? Would there be a punishment, and if so, how bad would it be?

I was thankful for the worries that circled my mind however, as it delayed the memory from just a few nights ago resurfacing – the last time I'd made my way through these halls and trekked up the narrow stairwell. As we stepped into her office, the scene from that night flashed in my head, but if I hadn't experienced it first-hand, I never would've guessed that something had gone down. Everything appeared to be in order and as I glanced towards the wall which Catherine had shot, I realized that a painting now hung over the spot where the bullet had hit.

"So," Catherine started, my attention moving to her as she took a seat at her desk, "do either of you want to explain what happened?"

I didn't want to be the one to admit that my temper and emotions had got the best of me, but as I kept quiet, so did Beckett. Sighing, I resolved to the fact that I'd have to tell the truth, but before I could get the first word out, Beckett interjected.

"It was my fault," he admitted, causing my eyes to whip towards him with shock. "I wasn't paying attention when I bumped into Aspen and her breakfast ended up going every-where. Others must've assumed I'd done it on purpose." He turned towards me as he trailed off, sending me a pointed look not to oppose the lie that slipped through his lips.

Turning back to face Catherine, I masked my surprise, though by the way she quirked her eyebrow and flicked her gaze between the two of us, I could tell that she didn't necessarily believe him.

"So you're saying that this was all a big misunderstanding?"

Beckett nodded, standing tall with his hands behind his back. "Yes."

She glanced to me once more, and while I nodded in agree-ment, I said nothing in response.

"Even if that may be," she started with authority, "I can't let this behaviour slide. If your accident somehow instigated the fight, I'm sorry, but that means that a large amount of the responsibility falls on your shoulders. I want you two to spend the day cleaning the Grand Hall." A small weight lifted off my chest, knowing that the punishment wasn't as severe as it could've been – though my relief came a moment too soon. "And tonight, I expect to see the both of you bunking outside, serving as an example to some of the other agents that these types of things will not be tolerated within this Division."

"Understood."

I blinked, thrown aback by the seemingly old-fashioned punishment, but noting the way that Beckett agreed so easily, I assumed it wasn't as bad as it could've been. "Understood," I repeated a few moments later, my voice holding less conviction than Beckett's had.

"Then you're both free to go."

On that cue I turned and headed for the door, feeling Catherine's gaze on my back, and when I didn't hear Beckett's footsteps following, I swung the door closed behind me.

"Is this what punishments are like around here?"

Hearing my words above the crackling of the fire, Beckett's gaze shifted towards me. "No," he said, "they're usually worse."

Now that was something I found hard to believe, though I was sure if I put the effort in, I would be able to think of worse things an agent could be tasked with.

The two of us had spent the day cleaning the Grand Hall from top to bottom, working around the agents that came in to eat and relax in between training sessions. It seemed as though every time we thought we'd finished, we noticed a spot on the ceiling or a new mess that had been made. The frustration built and exhaustion set in as the day dragged on, and once we were finally done, all I wanted to do was go back to my room and fall into my bed.

I couldn't do that however.

Beckett made quick work of directing me towards the storage closet where the Division stored their overnight equipment, pulling out a pile of blankets before leading me outside as the stars began to appear in the sky above. The weather was somewhat cooperative – giving us a clear night with no rain, however, the light chill that the wind carried was not so welcomed.

My surprise was evident when Beckett dropped his supplies next to one of the small barns situated on the back grounds, pulling at the door to reveal stacks of firewood. His skills were efficient in forming the base for a fire, and though I tried to help, I truly did nothing more than pass off logs and stoke the flames with kindling until they were tall enough to stand on their own.

Now, with the long, grueling hours behind us, the both of us lay on opposite sides of the fire, trying to find comfort on the uneven ground. A task that seemed impossible with nothing more than a few blankets in our disposal. Instead, I gave up trying and let my eyes scan over the star covered sky.

"Why did you take the fall for me?"

It was a question that'd been bothering me all day. He'd told Catherine that he'd bumped into me – which was true, but he had left out the aftermath that had truly initiated the food fight.

I heard Beckett shift underneath his blankets, and only when the rustling stopped did I shift my gaze from the stars above to him. "It wasn't that big of deal."

"That doesn't answer my question," I pointed out.

"Honestly, I was ticked off that I stayed up waiting for you last night in the training barn just for you to not show," he admitted. "I'd intended to confront you this morning, and when I bumped into you, I thought for a moment that you deserved it. When it set you off though, I realized you must've had something else on your mind."

The words were stab to my chest, knowing that I no doubt had let my emotions get the best of me. He hadn't done anything wrong or out of character, but my animosity towards Kira, Catherine, and Joe had been directed towards him. "And you're not going to ask what that was?"

He rolled back over, throwing me for a loop as he appeared to be mildly uninterested. "Not unless you want to tell me."

I didn't reply right away, letting silence sit between us, but it didn't take long for me to make a decision. I needed to get it off my chest – and if Beckett would listen, then I'd take advantage of the opportunity.

"It started the night of the alarm," I started, my voice vulnerable and just loud enough for Beckett to hear. "I was outside in the crowd when I noticed that everyone was shooting skeptical looks my way; as though I was at fault. It didn't make sense to me, but then Finn and Kira explained Catherine's past to me."

"You know, they likely aren't privy to anything more than the rumours that've been circulating since she was named Head of the Division," he cut in, letting me know he knew exactly what I was referring to.

I nodded. "Yeah, but I had to find out for myself. I made my way up to her office and had a front-row seat to watch her holding the leader of the Gemini Clan at gun point." I know I'd promised not to disclose the fact that Damon had been here, but if I'd learned one thing about Beckett, it was that he liked to operate alone. I didn't think I'd have to worry about him letting that fact slip. "She let him go, wanting to keep me safe, but when I left that night, there was a part of me that thought the rumours about her might be true."

I paused, expecting Beckett to have questions. To either rebuff my words or put in his own two cents, but as the lull in conversation lingered between us, I realized he wasn't going to speak up.

"Then yesterday afternoon, Kira led me to the room I used for training. Joe was there, and I thought nothing of the lie-detector they wanted to hook me up to, as Joe explained it was a lesson on remaining calm. What I didn't expect was an ambush." I breathed in a deep breath, releasing it slowly. "They hooked me up to the lie-detector, but also chained me to the chair before bringing Catherine in. They hadn't brought me there to train – they wanted me to confront my mom."

"So what happened?"

"She hooked herself up to the lie detector and had a reply for everything I asked, but that didn't mean I was ready to hear the answers."

"You know they work, right? The lie detectors. At least the ones that S.I.C.O use," he said. "So whatever Catherine told you, she was telling the truth."

"I know," I said, my voice wavering slightly. And that was part of the problem.

Beckett stayed quiet for a moment. "So are you mad that they were trying to help you, or mad because the only way they could get you to talk to Catherine was against your will?"

"Both," I replied confidently, before shaking my head as I second-guessed myself. "The latter..." I sighed. "I don't know."

"Maybe you should take some time to figure it out."

I couldn't find the words to reply, because I knew he was right. I couldn't continue to resent their actions, and I had to find a way to push past this and move forward.

Chapter 15

It wasn't quite morning as I opened my eyes. In the distance, I could see a pink tint lighting up the skyline as the stars began to fade. With the sun gracing the horizon, I nuzzled underneath the blankets, only to push myself upwards when I realized that I was in a more comfortable position than I'd been the night before.

There was a chill to the air as my eyes scanned the area where Beckett and I had fallen asleep. The remnants of the fire that had burned between us lay extinguished on the ground beside me, and even though it couldn't have been later than six in the morning, the spot where I expected to find Beckett was empty. It was only when I let my gaze drop to my own lap that I realized the blankets he'd used were now lumped on top of mine.

My eyebrows drew together, knowing that at some point during the night he must've gotten up to quell the fire, and wondering why, at presumably the same time, he'd give up the little comfort he'd had for me – the same person who'd gotten him stuck with this punishment in the first place.

It was times like this that I noticed that there were two sides to his personality. Most of the time, it appeared as though he didn't care about much other than himself and doing his job, but in rare moments, his walls disappeared to reveal someone who was thoughtful, caring, and easy to talk to.

However, I knew there was no use trying to figure out how his mind worked first thing in the morning, so I let it go, making a mental note to thank him the next time I saw him.

As I stood up, piling the blankets into my arms, my eyes caught onto a folded piece of paper wedged underneath the blanket that I'd been using as a make-shift pillow. Crouching down, I placed the blankets down to the side and picked up the note. Unfolding it, a small smile twitched at my lips as I read what was written.

I'll be in the training barn late tonight if you still want to learn how to protect yourself.

Relief coursed through me, hoping that this short message meant that yesterday was behind us. The physical aspect of my training needed work, and if, after everything that had transpired yesterday, he was still willing to help me, I wasn't going to turn it down.

Tucking the note into my back pocket, I resumed cleaning up. Once the charred fire logs were disposed of and the dirty blankets were tossed down the communal laundry chute, I nipped into the Grand Hall. Those who were up this early eyed me cautiously, probably waiting for a repeat of the previous morning to occur, but I paid them little attention. Grabbing a coffee and a breakfast burrito, I didn't linger, instead making my way up to my room.

The concept of weekends didn't exist at Division 27. It didn't matter if it was Tuesday afternoon, Friday night or Sunday morning – training still went on and assignments were still given out. However, with no arrangements to train with Joe today, I used the time go over what I'd learned over the past couple of weeks. It was necessary, I felt like, as my mind had been all over the place as of late, but as the hours wore on, I found my concentration slipping bit by bit.

Instead, I thought of Kira and the current predicament the two of us were in. Unless she was incredibly skilled at masking her true emotions – which was entirely possible, she had seemed genuinely apologetic both the day she'd left me sitting with Catherine and Joe and when she'd cornered me in the Grand Hall the previous morning. Before yesterday, I hadn't wanted to give her the benefit of the doubt, but Beckett's advice now had me thinking differently.

Was I angry with her because of what she'd done?

Yes.

Was I angry that I hadn't really had a choice in confronting my mom?

Yes.

But, after the fact, I knew both her and Joe were trying to help me, and I couldn't be angry at them for that. They were only looking out for me.

When it became evidently clear that my productivity was shot – my focus continuously straying to the small amount of guilt in the pit of my stomach, I sighed. Pushing my things to the side, I stood up from my spot at the top of my bed and headed for the door.

It was closing in on five as I stood in front of the lab. Typing in the five-digit code for the door, I pulled it open once the light shone green. Both the sound of the door opening and my footsteps caused Kira's gaze to lift from what she was focused on. Offering her a hesitant smile as I hovered just inside the doorway, I cringed internally as she showed no response to my presence, simply turning her focus back to what she'd been working on.

This was going to be slightly harder than I'd expected.

"Hey," I spoke up, clearing my throat. "Can we talk?"

"I'm kind of busy," she replied.

Ouch. "It'll only take a minute." She leant back from the computer she was using and looked my way, and though she said nothing, a simple nod of the head gave me the go-ahead. "I guess I just wanted to say that I was sorry... for not letting you explain your side of things. I was upset about the situation, and because you were a part of it, my anger shifted to you."

"Aspen," she started, "maybe you didn't see how bad the situation between you and Catherine was, but I could. You couldn't so much as talk about her without some sort of animosity in your voice, and it was like every time something involved her, you acted out of instinct instead of thinking things through. Letting your emotions rule your decisions can be dangerous. Trust me."

There was an underlying tone to her words that I could remember hearing on a few occasions since I'd met her – always when we were talking about her position in the Divi-sion, her past, or ways for me to stay safe. If I could guess, I'd bet that whatever was being left unsaid had to do with the real reason she'd made the switch from fieldwork to the lab. It could've be one decision or one mistake that'd ended with major consequences, and though the curiosity was there, I didn't push for answers.

"And I'm sorry that I agreed to Joe's idea before talking with you," she continued. "I wanted to help, but I know that it wasn't exactly the best way to do so."

"You think?" I quirked an eyebrow, watching as a sheepish look crossed her face before I sighed. "But you were both right – I did need to talk with Catherine. I might not have been ready, but I think I needed that push. I was being stubborn and was fixated on the fact that, in my mind, she was the reason I was stuck in the middle of everything."

Kira was quiet for a moment, regarding me with a questioning gaze. "And now? Is that still what you think?"

"It's complicated." I didn't want to have to go into the complications of it all – Damon, his plan, the weapons. "But I know that it's not her I have to worry about going forward."

"Then that's a good thing, right?"

"In some ways," I replied vaguely, nodding my head. Letting my gaze wander, it settled on the set-up she'd been working with when I'd walked in. It was more than just a computer like I'd first thought. There was a file stocked full of papers lying on the work surface, as well as a device that was hooked up to the computer that enclosed a small volume of chemicals. My eyebrows furrowed in interest. "What are you working on?"

Her lips pressed together as apprehensiveness flitted across her features. A sign of confliction as she debated whether to tell me the truth.

"A few years ago, S.I.C.O was funding a project that Division 27 was highly invested in," she started, her words slow. "We were the main contributors and the research that was being done had been extensive, but the project was abruptly cut just over two years ago. According to what I've been told, the data and equipment hasn't been touched since then." Kira reached across the work table to grab the file. "That is, until Catherine spoke to me and a few of the other lab technicians after the alarm, wanting us to open the project back up."

She didn't object as I grabbed the file from her and flipped it open. Most of the document were filled with meaningless scrawls and data, the level of complexity more than I could understand. "What is all of this?" I asked as I lifted my gaze back up to meet hers.

"The project is called invisibilis." My eyes widened marginally with surprise. "Previously, the Division was testing out material modifications that could alter the way visible wavelengths are seen."

"So they were..."

"In the beginning stages of creating a functioning invisibility cloak," she finished for me. Her lips twitched up at the sides as my mouth opened to form words that couldn't find their way out. "That's pretty much what my reaction was too." She took the file back from me as she nodded to the device hooked up to the computer. "The research was just beginning to show conclusive results when it was shut down years ago, but now, with the advances in technology growing day by day, we're being careful with how we move forward with this."

My mind immediately jumped to the consequences of what could happen if this information ended up in the wrong hands. An unsettling feeling crept up my spine. "Do you know why Catherine chose now to open this project back up?"

My voice was an octave lower than usual and shaking slightly with worry. My apprehension wasn't lost on Kira, frowning as she replied, "I think you already know the answer to that."

I gulped, realizing that I did.

It was because there was a fight coming, whether we chose to admit it or not, and she wanted to have every option at her disposal to make sure the Division didn't take a hit.

Later that night, I stood in the middle of the training barn with Beckett's arm wrapped my neck, though not tight enough to hurt me. His position behind me kept me faced away from him as he coached me on how to escape it.

"When you're in this position, the best strategy is to protect your airway by gripping the attacker's arm, tuck your chin into the crook of their elbow, and to utilize your feet to try and knock them off balance," he said.

I brought my hands up and positioned myself as he said. With my back pressing tightly against his chest, I maneuvered my right foot behind his, locking his leg between mine before turning around and trying my best to push him to the ground. Even with my momentum, he didn't budge much, but he did seem partially impressed that I had executed the move properly.

"That was good," he nodded, slipping his arm from my grip as he took a step back. "Your technique is improving, but since your opponents will likely be my size or larger in the field, the important thing to work on is your strength. You'll need to be able to throw them off slightly so that you can take the opportunity to escape."

Letting out a deep breath, I nodded. "So are we working on my strength next, then?" I asked, my breathing a little heavier than normal.

"I actually think it's about time to pack it in for the night," he said, lifting his eyebrow as if to challenge me.

In all honesty, tonight's training session had been highly productive. Beckett had known that I wanted to work on both protecting myself and being able to protect others; the former of which he'd decided to focus on for the past hour. We'd gone through high intensity drills that were meant to sharpen my senses and keep me quick on my feet. An agility course, an interval training circuit, and a set of hand-eye co-ordination exercises – I got through them all, but not before working up a sweat as we switched over to more practical exercises.

"Tired already?" I teased.

He rolled his eyes and a small smirk appeared on his lips. "I'm sure you'd like to think that," he drawled, "but considering I'm leaving for an assignment at six, I want to grab a few hours of sleep."

I could feel my features shift marginally with surprise. It was already going on one in the morning. "We could've put off the training until tomorrow. I wouldn't have minded."

"Don't worry about it." He shook his head. "I'm used to having a scattered sleep schedule; it's kind of hard not to be."

I nodded, though I didn't have a response. Instead, the two of us made quick work of cleaning up the training barn, and within minutes were stepping out into the night air side by side. Waiting as he pulled the door to the barn shut, I let my gaze fall over the empty grounds.

I was so used to the constant state of action that Division 27 seemed to thrive on. Agents coming and going at all hours of the day, partners prepping for their upcoming assignments, a continuous desire to train and improve upon skills – it was the ongoing hustle that seemed to keep everyone going. Sometimes, however, I forgot what it felt like to be in a state of peace.

But in that moment, where everything was settled and not a person was in sight, I felt a sense of calmness wash over me.

"Are you coming?"

Turning my head, I saw Beckett standing a few feet away from me, a curious expression on his face. "You go ahead," I said, my eyes flitting back towards the trees that lined the grounds, "I'll be in soon."

He lifted a brow. "Not thinking of running away again, are you?"

Whereas a month ago I would've found his words patronizing, there was now a light undertone that told me he was only teasing. "No," I mused. "Not tonight."

For a second, it seemed as though he was going to say something more, but decided against it at the last minute. Instead, he nodded in acceptance before turning his back to me and making his way towards the nearest entrance alone.

Making my way across the grounds, the only thing that could be heard was the low whistling of the wind and the soft rustle of the leaves. The combination of the silence and the solidarity in the moment was almost intoxicating to me; the familiar atmosphere of a life I'd since left behind. In the back of my mind I knew that it was likely someone was on patrol, currently watching my every move, but I couldn't find it in me to care. It was a breath of fresh air and a break in routine I hadn't known I'd desperately needed.

I took my time – no real course to my steps as I circled the grounds. Nothing was out of place or unexpected; everything just as I'd seen it several times over the past month.

Except for when it wasn't.

It was a small flicker of light that caught my eye as I glanced to my left, just bright enough to cast its glare through a narrow opening in the trees. My brows furrowed as I squinted, attempting to make sense of what it was. It was dim, and coming from the ground, the discovery of which caused me to release a bated breath, figuring it was unlikely to be an intruder who was waiting to strike.

Was it some sort of security system I hadn't noticed before? A flashlight that someone had left abandoned earlier in the evening?

Whatever it was, it wasn't that far away. Maybe ten meters at most, and with my curiosity winning out over what should've been a sound judgement call to turn and walk away, I threw a glance over my shoulder before moving towards the light source.

My steps were slow and as I maneuvered through the trees, their tall structures acting as a shield against the cool night winds, my heart rate sped up. It was almost as if my subconscious knew that I was stumbling across something that I shouldn't be.

Something that didn't belong.

Because the light wasn't coming from something that had been dropped. No. My eyes grew in surprise and my movements halted as I realized it was coming from underground.

It was glowing in the shape of a square, strangely less prominent now that I stood above it. Intrigued, I crouched, my knees hitting the uneven forest floor as I pushed away the leaves and dirt. It was less than a minute later when my hand hit what I was looking for – cement. With more urgency than before, I uncovered the rest of the cement block before sitting back on my heels to take it all in.

The light was seeping out of the sides of the block, making it prevalent that it was being used as a cover. But for what? The only indentation on the cement was an 'X' with a few lines etched around it, which did nothing to spark a clue in my memory as to what could be hidden underneath.

As I dug my fingers into the dirt beside it and pushed, I was surprised when the cement shifted sideways by just a few inches. With new determination, I used all the strength I had to keep pushing, causing my breath to catch in the back of my throat as the light grew brighter and a large hole was unveiled.

A hole large enough for someone to drop down into.

Locating the source of the light – a torch that had been left hanging on the wall of the underground tunnel that opened at the base of the hole, I made a split-second decision. Swinging my legs out from underneath me, I braced my hands on the edge and inched my body into the hole. And then I let go, my feet hitting the ground seconds later with a low thud.

The smell of pine scented trees was immediately masked with the stale air that filled the tunnel. It was damp, and despite the glare from the torch that now hung next to me, it was pitch black. An eerie feeling crept up my spine as I looked down the long path in front of me, and even though I could've made the choice to climb back up, I wanted to investigate.

Grabbing the torch, I held it out in front of me as I wandered further into the tunnel, and the deeper I went, the more I got the sense that this place had, up until recently, been long forgotten. There was a mixture of soil and cement beneath my feet, stopping my steps from echoing down the corridor, and with cobwebs covering nearly every surface, I couldn't help but notice the way that some of the ones overhead had been torn away from the relatively low hanging ceilings.

And then, as I approached a turn in the tunnel, the sudden sound of someone else's movements hit my ears and the reality of the situation caught up to me. I was snooping in a place I didn't belong and I wasn't alone.

As I rounded the corner however, I breathed a sigh of relief. "Finn?"

I expected him to be startled, considering I'd found him at the end of an underground tunnel in the middle of the night, but when he lifted his head and met my gaze, the surprise that he was no longer alone faded quickly, morphing into a smile. "Hey," he greeted. "I see you've found one of the Division's many hideaways."

The cheeriness that naturally rolled off him didn't seem appropriate in our current situation. In fact, it was the first time since I'd met him that his emotions didn't seem genuine, but a mask for something else. His eyes were vacant, his posture a little too straight, and his grin too wide.

Something was off.

"Yeah," I drawled, taking a few careful steps forward as my eyes swept over the room. "What exactly is this place?"

There were bookshelves lining the walls that looked like they hadn't been touched in years; cobwebs and dust covering them in a thick film. The same went for the old paintings and the broken clock that seemed to be stuck with both of its hands pointing towards the faded number four – all of which hung on the walls, looking like they were one touch away from falling to the ground. This was a contrast to the equipment that filled the table that separated Finn and I. The computer, while an ancient model, was booted up and currently running through some sort of program too advanced for me to understand while numerous files, seemingly new, were filled with papers stacked every which way.

"It's an underground record room that S.I.C.O used to store files back in the day," he explained, pausing to type out a command for the program. "I found it a few years ago, but lately I've been using it to try and find anything that can help us."

"Against the Gemini Clan?" He nodded in response, though as the program continued to run, the more his attention seemed to be drawn to it. I grabbed one of the files off the table, opening it and scanning through the papers. "Well, have you found anything yet?"

"I haven't been able to find much other than old cases that have been closed for ages or names of agents that are long since gone."

"I'm sure there's something here," I said, trying to be optimistic as I reached to grab another file. "We can just – "

The rest of my words died in my throat as Finn reached out and grabbed my hand, shaking his head. "It's getting late," he said, watching as the program he was working on ran to completion. As it did so, he quickly removed the memory stick he had hooked up and stuck it in his pocket. "I need to get up early for a meeting with Catherine, and I don't want to leave you out here alone." His voice was sincere as he shut down the computer before rounding the table to stand next to me. "Come on, I'll walk you back."

Maybe I wouldn't have picked up on his diversion tactic if I hadn't just come from a training session with Beckett, whose warning about Finn from weeks ago suddenly jumped to the forefront of my thoughts.

I just don't fully trust him.

And in that moment, I wasn't sure if I did either. He seemed too rushed – wanting to keep whatever he was doing private, and even if it wasn't something to be concerned about, it was enough to suggest something out of the ordinary was going on.

But I kept my suspicions to myself, not wanting to make any waves. Instead I nodded, falling into stride with him as we headed back down the tunnel.

Chapter 16

It felt as though the following week passed in the blink of an eye.

Having put any feelings of animosity behind me, I had multiple training sessions scheduled with Joe, who worked with me to sharpen my mental abilities when it came to thinking in the field. This included lessons on how to smartly tail someone, which common places made the best spots to place bugs, and how to spot when I was under surveillance. Each lesson was in depth, including previous cases to study and hypothetical situations in which he expected me to run through a play by play of how I'd handle different hardships.

On top of that, I was spending time with Kira in the lab, working on my French, and meeting up with Beckett almost nightly for training sessions. Everything was becoming routine, and it felt like I barely had a spare minute to breathe.

However, through it all, the one thing that prodded at the back of my mind was Finn. The morning after finding him deep underground, I had wanted to talk to him about it. I hadn't wanted to confront him per se, I was just looking for some sort of reassurance that my suspicions about him weren't warranted.

But it didn't take me long to figure out that he was avoiding me.

The first clue came that first morning when, as I stood in line for breakfast in the Grand Hall, I noticed Finn get up from a table across the room and make his way out into the hallway. I tried to follow him, but by the time I reached the hall, he was already long gone.

He pulled the same disappearing act two more times that day, and continuously as the days wore on. With each day that passed, I struggled to hold back my frustration while going about my day as though nothing had changed, even though it had.

I could no longer trust Finn, and though I wasn't yet jumping to the worst-case scenario, my mind was going haywire at the possibilities. Whatever he was doing, he clearly wanted to keep it private, but not wanting to make a big deal about something that could end up being nothing more than a high security assignment, I decided it was best not to tell anyone about my suspicions. Not yet.

After all, for the moment, all I had was an uneasy feeling in my gut to go off.

Strangely enough, the only thing that succeeded in distracting me from the chaos inside my head were the nights I spent training with Beckett. When his schedule permitted, he would spend an hour or two working with me – sharpening my skills and narrowing down the technical aspects of self-defense, and even though it hadn't been all that long, I could tell that his lessons were making a difference.

It'd only been once so far that he'd mentioned having to go on a late-night stakeout, therefore canceling our usual meet-up, which was why, when I walked into the training barn just after midnight on a Thursday night to find the space empty, my forehead creased with a mixture of confusion and concern.

Beckett was always the first one here, mainly because he'd normally have spent the majority of the hours leading up to our lessons working on his own abilities. He was nothing if not dedicated, which made it all the more worrying that he was late.

Not wanting to sit around and waste time, I grabbed a pair of gloves from the pile to my right before getting into a fighting stance in front of one of the training bags to warm-up. The first punch I threw was a standard jab, and from there I went through a quick combination of hits each time the bag came back towards me. After every combination, I took a quick breather, stretching out my arms before going at it again, and when I finally stepped back twenty minutes later, Beckett was still nowhere to be seen.

I stood, breathing heavily and gulping down water from the bottle I'd brought, wondering why he hadn't shown up. It was unlikely that he forgot, or that he was out on another assignment, as he should've just returned –

And that was when my curiosity collided with my fear, opening a pit of uneasiness in my stomach.

From what I knew, he'd been out on assignment all day, however I wasn't privy to the details of what he'd been working on. I didn't know if he'd gone out alone or alongside others, and I could only assume that whatever his assignment had been, it had been important. And dangerous.

Letting my bottle drop to the floor, I didn't give my movements a second thought as I spun on my heel and headed back towards the main building. Using the nearest entrance, I weaved my way through the halls, trying my best not to draw the attention of the agents that were tasked with patrolling for the night.

I only knew which room belonged to Beckett because, one morning a few weeks back, I'd gotten up before the crack of dawn and had been headed downstairs at the same time he'd been leaving for an assignment. It was one on the corner of an otherwise deserted hall, but I guess for someone who liked his privacy, it was perfect.

When I finally reached his room, I noted the fact that no light could be seen from the crack underneath the door, but nevertheless, I brought my hand up to knock. The sound of my knuckles rapping against the door echoed down the hall and I cringed, lightening the force as I knocked again a few moments later.

Moving from foot to foot, my worries began to grow as the seconds passed and the lights stayed off, even though I knew there could realistically be several places he could be if not in bed. Just as I was about turn away, hearing no hints of movement from the other side of the door, it swung open unexpectedly, with the lights following quickly after.

My eyes widened as I took in Beckett, who stood there with wet hair, no shirt on, and a pair of baggy sweatpants hanging almost indecently low on his hips. The daily training and the commitment he made to his position within the Division appeared to have suited him well, because as my gaze trailed slowly down his body, I took note of every inch of solid muscle.

When I found myself following the trail of hair that ran downwards from his navel, disappearing beneath his pants, I snapped my head back up to meet his eyes – figuring it was a safer place for the time being.

"Sorry," I said, clearing my throat in an effort to appear less flustered than I was. It appeared to me that he hadn't taken notice of my wandering eyes, which I was thankful for as I continued. "I know it's late – I just – you didn't show up for training, and I wanted to make sure you were okay."

Dragging a hand through his damp hair, he sighed. "Yeah, sorry about that," he apologized, gesturing me inside his room as he stepped aside. The few steps I took were cautious, though when he let the door close behind me, the tension in my shoulders slowly began to fade. "Things didn't exactly go as planned today, and I just got back about twenty minutes ago."

"You were gone all day?" I asked gently, surprise lacing my words.

He nodded, and as I took another look at him, I noticed the little things that I'd previously overlooked. There were lines etched into his face that alluded to how tired he was, as well as plenty of new bruises that roughed up his skin. "Yeah," he said in a low tone. "And I figured that since I didn't show, you'd have already gone to bed."

"Yeah, well, you know what they say about people who assume," I trailed, the corners of my lips twitching upwards.

A tired laugh left his lips as he shook his head in thinly veiled amusement. "Fair enough Rigby."

As a comfortable silence settled around us, I took the chance to glance around the room. It wasn't much different from my own. Nothing but a bed and a wardrobe, though there was a small bookshelf which had been placed in the corner, filled to the brim with an array of small binders, folders, and the odd paperback. I did find it peculiar, however, that Beckett's room held no personal touches. He'd lived here for years – since right after his parents had died, and to have done nothing to mark the space as his own in all that time, I felt a small stab of sympathy for the way his life had turned out.

The thing was, even with how closed off he was, I knew that Beckett was grateful for S.I.C.O, and for Catherine, as they'd taken him in when he'd had nowhere else to go.

"So, is there any chance you're going to clue me in on what you've been working on lately?" I asked, quirking an eyebrow as my gaze fell back to Beckett.

His features softened marginally, and just as I expected, he shook his head. "If I told you – "

"Let me guess," I mused, "you'd have to kill me?"

There was a seriousness that sparked in his eyes. "No Aspen," he said, pausing for a moment. "If I told you, I'd be worried about you doing something that could get you killed."

"Do you understand?" Joe asked the next day as I sat across from him in our usual meeting room.

It wasn't our normal lesson though. Over the last hour, Joe had been having me sort through old cases that hadn't ended so well. There'd been undercover identities that had been leaked, situations where agents had made dire mistakes while out in the field, and worst of all, a few assignments that had ended where the agents hadn't made it out alive.

The point of revisiting the past – at least in Joe's eyes – was to learn from it, which I could understand. It was why I'd paid close attention and worked through each scenario with him throughout our lesson, wanting to take in all the information I could.

As I nodded in response to his question, he began packing things away. Our time was up, and while I didn't normally make a habit of lingering around afterwards, this time I had something I needed to ask him. Something that had been weighing on my mind for quite a while now.

"Actually, do you have a few more minutes?" I asked, biting my lip anxiously.

"Sure," he replied, stopping what he was doing as he lifted an eyebrow. "What's up?"

I took in a deep breath, waiting a few beats before I asked, "would you be able to tell me a bit more about the Gemini Clan?"

Although he tried to remain unfazed as the words rolled off my tongue, I noticed his gaze sharpen and his shoulders tense just marginally. "What do you want to know?" he asked after a prolonged pause, his words stiff with worry about what I'd say next.

"I know Catherine said that one of the weapons they're after is hidden here in the Division," I said, and before he could cut in, I quickly continued. "But there are others, right? Are S.I.C.O taking measures to protect the rest of them?"

"Aspen," he started slowly, causing an ounce of dread to spread through my veins. "Your mother wasn't completely honest with you – not as much as she could have been. Yes, the founders of S.I.C.O crafted numerous weapons back in the day – most of which were scattered across the globe when things started to go downhill within the inner ranks, but there are only four that the Gemini Clan are interested in." He paused for a moment. "One was destroyed years ago, one was given to a CIA division and another to a MI6 division to guard, while the final one was trusted to our Division."

There was a foreboding tone to his words. "Okay," I trailed off, a crease of confusion forming above my brows. I felt like I was missing an important part of the puzzle. "Then why does it feel like keeping ours safe is so imperative?"

I noticed the way his fists tightened and the way his jaw tightened before he spoke. "The Gemini Clan is already in possession of both the other weapons." My intake of breath was sharp. "It was last year, around October." He paused. "Do you remember the cases I had you read when you first arrived? The unexplained breaking and entering charges?"

My eyes widened in realization.

"Those specific cases – the ones that had to do with government intel – they were altered. The real case files are locked up. Two of the logged break-ins targeted the CIA and MI6 on the same night, and while both organizations had successfully guarded the weapon they were in charge of for years, neither of them knew they were under attack until it was too late."

It took me a few moments to process what he was saying, and when I spoke again, my voice quivered. "You're telling me... the Gemini Clan... they already possess two of the three remaining weapons? That the only one left is the one hidden here?" Joe nodded solemnly. "And no one thought to tell me?"

"It wasn't just you," he replied insistently. "None of the trainees know about it. We didn't want to be the cause of any unnecessary worry."

"It wouldn't be unnecessary! I'm in the middle of all of this, so if I'm in danger, I want to know. And, given the choice, I'm sure all the other trainees would feel the same way." I could feel my temper rising the more I spoke. "What if another attack is being planned right this minute?"

"Aspen – "

"You yourself thought that someone within the Division could be working with the Gemini Clan," I pointed out. "So if someone is working for them, how can you be sure that the weapon hidden here is still secure?"

He stood then, trying to exude authority as he looked down at me. "I'm really not at liberty to discuss this with you Aspen."

"But can't you even – "

The next words caught in my throat as a familiar siren – with three consecutive alarms – sounded loudly around us.

No.

Not again.

While my initial reaction was to freeze at the sudden overhead noise, it was only another moment before I sprang to my feet. Looking to Joe for guidance, my features bright with panic, I saw that his face had drained of colour. He snapped out of it quickly however, pushing down his fear as he got down to business.

As he turned his back towards me, rummaging through the shelves in search of something, I was the first one to speak. "What do we do?" I asked, my eyes tracking his every move.

Pulling a key from the mess and slipping it into his pocket, he turned back towards me, bending down to grab a hold of the gun he kept in the holster around his ankle. "You can follow the crowds Aspen. Get to safety."

I was just about to object when, suddenly, the door to the room was thrown open.

Both our gazes snapped towards the entryway, and I felt the smallest amount of relief course through me as I saw Catherine standing there. With everything going on lately, I hadn't found the time to talk to her, but I was surprised, in the moment, to feel nothing in the realm of animosity or anger. In fact, I felt empowered. All I wanted to do in that moment was help, in any way that I could.

"Joe, you need to get to the cellars," she said, leaving no room for discussion. "Now."

"On it," he replied, not sparing me another glance as he pushed passed me and disappeared out of sight.

"Come on," she said urgently, "we need to go."

Stepping out into the hallway, the chaos seemed to be slightly more organized than the last time. The younger agents were still struck with worry, moving around without a clue, but the older ones – the ones who I assumed Catherine had briefed extensively with protocols over the last few weeks, seemed more calm. More in control.

The evacuation protocol was different this time however, and it was only then that I realized the alarm was slightly different than the last one. There was something off with the rhythm of the sirens, and while they still rang loudly in rounds of three, it was to alert us of something much more frightening.

Last time the alarm had been set off by my father, or possibly other agents of the Gemini Clan as they breached the Division's outer security. This, however, wasn't just a breach in security. This was a breach within the walls of the Division itself – a failed attempt at breaking into the highly classified areas.

I pushed down the unsettling feeling that began to brew in the pit of my stomach, figuring that, while up until this point it had only been an educated guess, it was now highly likely that someone within the Division was using their position to aid the agents of the Gemini Clan.

It made sense then, that instead of gathering out on the grounds, the agents in charge of security were not allowing anyone to leave. We were going into full lock-down mode.

As we passed the staircase that led up to the housing wing, Catherine stopped for a moment, her eyes meeting mine as she gave her directions. "Get to your room Aspen, and make sure you stay safe."

Though it was an order, there was a whisper of worry that laced her words. She was trying to protect me, that I understood, but the way I looked at it, I hadn't truly been safe since my birthday.

So, I didn't listen. I wanted to do more than sit around and wait.

As Catherine shifted her attention back to the situation at hand, I wasn't sure if she even realized that I was following her. Her focus was zeroed in on making sure that every measure of security we had was in place. Moving through the crowd, she stopped for only seconds at a time to give orders to those agents who held seniority before moving on.

It took great effort to keep up with her, but each step fueled my adrenaline further. When we rounded a corner, heading into a section of the building I hadn't yet explored, it was noticeably less chaotic, as there were no trainees to be seen. There were agents that stood in front of each door – their eyes following each step we took. They'd been taught to catch every movement, whether suspicious or not, and if the guns in their hands were anything to go by, they were prepared for the worst.

Distracted momentarily by their presence, I fell behind, but as I sped up to catch Catherine, I reached for her arm, pulling her to a stop. I stood my ground as she turned to look at me. "I want to help," I said firmly. "Just tell me what to do."

I had pushed her into a corner, because in our current situation, there wasn't a spare second for her to think about anything but making sure everyone was safe and the building was secure.

"Okay," she conceded, gesturing me to follow her. "Come on, we've got to be quick."

There was no time to ask questions as she turned on her heel and marched straight into the madness with me right behind her.

Chapter 17

I t was clear what Catherine's objective was – to secure the building and to make sure that nothing had been compromised.

This consisted of asking each agent we passed for a report on who'd been the last people given access to the secure areas, as well as inspecting each room to see if anything was out of place. It was a lot all at once; trying to absorb every little thing she did, as well as take note of the names that the agents gave up.

None of the names however, stood out to me as suspicious, though it wasn't lost on me that sometimes the ones who seemed loyal could be the ones who delivered the deepest betrayal. There weren't free passes given out for being in the right place at the wrong time. Anyone could be guilty until proven innocent.

Once every room was checked and we reached the corner of what appeared to be a dead-end hallway, Catherine finally halted in her pursuit and turned to me. "I know you want to be a part of all of this," she started, "but what comes next is bigger than just you and me, and I can't let you get caught up in this any more than you already have."

There was a surge of determination that burned inside of me. "I know you think – "

"This isn't my call, Aspen," she spoke sternly, cutting me off. "There are rules. Ones that need to be followed in cases like this. It doesn't matter if you're willing to step up and fight; it's a matter of protecting the greater good, and you're not skilled enough to do that."

There was a part of me that wanted to protest her blatant dismissal of how hard I'd worked since I'd gotten here – of how much of myself I'd put into this Division, but the rest of me knew better. I knew that I still had a long way to go. That I was still considered an amateur, and would be for a long time to come. The problem however, was that the most important lesson I'd learned over the past few weeks was to be prepared, because without considering every variable, there were too many places for things go wrong.

Something that Catherine seemed hell-bent on depriving me and many of the agents of. If we didn't know exactly what we were up against, how could we be expected to help when the time came?

"Is it not better to be prepared?" I asked, voicing my inner thoughts. "To know what we're facing and strategize the best plan of attack?"

"You don't understand." There was something about the way she looked, almost pleadingly, at me that caused any further objections to die in my throat. "As much as I want to explain the specifics, I can't risk it. Not after today."

It didn't take long for everything to fit together – for me to understand what she was really trying to say. There were too many things that could go wrong if Catherine were to announce to the Division what was truly going on. Too many things could backfire.

In these times of uncertainty, trust wasn't something she could easily give away.

Information could only be revealed on a need to know basis, as the risk of giving out intel to the wrong person was high.

As we stood there in silence, her eyes on wide alert for any miniscule clue as to who had been behind the breach, question after question popped into my head. I was desperate for answers. Who did she think, in the Division, had betrayed her? What was their plan? Why were they sitting back while, day by day, the Gemini Clan was only growing stronger?

But it was clear that it wasn't the time for answers.

"All clear."

I whipped my head around at the unexpected voice to see Joe walking purposefully towards us, and other than the fact that his jaw was clenched tight, he appeared to be calm and collected – the opposite of what I was feeling. In fact, as his strides came to a halt beside me, he couldn't have looked more in his element.

"Where did you come from?" I asked, the words slipping through my lips before I could stop them. Though they might as well have fell on deaf ears as he paid me no attention, keeping his gaze solely on Catherine.

"Nothing was out of place? There was no hint of forced entry?"

"Not at first glance," Joe replied. "I'll gather a few agents and go down there again once everything calms down to scope it out, but right now, everything is safe."

Catherine gave a curt nod in response, and when Joe made a move to turn and walk away, I stepped in front of him. "This is about the weapon, right?" I asked. "You're saying it's still safely hidden?"

His gaze drifted over my shoulder momentarily before meeting my eyes. "I'm sorry Aspen, but you don't have the clearance to know anything more than you already do," he said matter-of-factly. "Now come on, you can help me shut down this alarm."

"But what about – "

My voice trailed off however, because as I turned back to look at Catherine, there was nothing to see but an empty dead-end hallway. She was gone.

When the alarm ceased and things began to return to normal, I wasn't the only one looking for answers. While the senior agents remained tight-lipped on the assignments they were given, the junior agents and trainees, like myself, were left to sit and wonder what was going on.

There'd been two alarms so far, and as the days passed with no hint as to what the plan was going forward, the fear of the unknown began to linger over the Division. Some agents took to moving about the halls in groups, feeling safer with numbers, while others distanced themselves from the increased sense of panic, not knowing who they could trust. Whichever category they fell into however, it didn't seem as though anyone wanted to tread in the unknown waters that laid ahead.

They were like sitting ducks – just waiting to get hit.

But I couldn't just sit back and do nothing. I wanted to help, and the only way I could think to do so without interfering was to investigate on my own.

Whenever I found myself with an hour to spare, I slipped away to the library, wanting to learn more about the history of S.I.C.O, the Gemini Clan, and the weapons that they were supposedly after. It started out as a way to fill the scattered holes in my mind – all of which were found within a puzzle of information that happened to be missing a few important pieces, and with each new passage I read, I felt a small thrill knowing that I was getting closer to seeing the full picture.

It was the knowledge that I craved above all else.

I read pages on the founders. How they'd teamed up in the late 19th century, after leaving the CIA and MI6, to form a new brand of covert operations. One that was still concerned with taking down criminals, but was stripped of government expectation. There'd been a scientific genius, two world-class combat fighters, and one who'd perfected the art of being a world-class spy.

As the years went by, they'd expanded the team when necessary, but what Catherine had failed to mention on my first night here was that, when she'd said one of their own had turned on them, she meant that the trader had taken it upon himself to murder one of the founders.

I held back a flinch as I read... 'On the brink of a scientific breakthrough, the body of Robert Adley had been found in his lab with several lacerations to the skin, later found to be the work of Jeffery Morton – the standing head of Division 13.'

Jeffery Morton.

I read over his name several times, searching every crevice of my memory for a link to the name, but nothing came up. Yet another dead-end.

Closing the book in frustration, I pushed out of my chair, ignoring the narrowed looks I received as the legs squeaked against the floor, and headed to the far right of the library where I knew the old Divisional records were kept. There were several binded books for every Division, each one con-taining copies of dated assignment reports, milestones, and important documents – but as I'd noticed before, there was only one book pertaining to Division 13.

Having previously skimmed through it, I knew there was nothing but a few founding documents and completed mis-sion reports. Nevertheless, I pulled it from the shelf and returned to my seat, hoping that I'd missed something small. Something important.

Sadly, the deeper I looked into the pages, it was evident that there was nothing for me to have missed.

Slamming the book closed with frustration, I sighed, clos-ing my eyes as I tried to figure out my next move. There were only so many resources available to me, and with each day that passed, the pool of information appeared to be drying up quickly.

As I opened my eyes seconds later, my shoulders sagged with defeat, figuring I'd need a break to regroup. It was when

I reached out to grab the book again, wanting to return it to its shelf before retiring to my room for the night, that I saw it.

A small design marked into the bottom of the back jacket.

The closer I looked, I realized it wasn't just any old design, but a symbol – one that I'd seen before. An X with a line on both sides as well as the top. It was the same symbol that'd been marked on the cement block that had given way to the underground hideaway where I'd found Finn.

Though now that I was seeing the symbol again, I realized they weren't just lines. They were roman numerals. Three ones and an X – standing for the number ten – adding up to thirteen.

A thrill shot through me, knowing that I'd finally stumbled upon a missing piece of the puzzle, but the feeling of victory was quickly overshadowed by that of fear. I could feel the hair on the nape of my neck standing on end as a chill crept down my spine. If this was indeed what I thought it was – an unofficial symbol for Division 13 – then I couldn't keep quiet any longer about what I'd seen that night I'd found Finn.

Even if he wasn't the one who'd triggered the alarm a few nights ago, even if he wasn't mixed up with the Gemini Clan, I'd found him in a compromising position and now had proof, even if it was small, that it may not have been as innocent as he wanted me to believe.

Tightening my grip on the book, I stood up and turned towards the library's entrance in a hurry. I could've went straight to the top – to my mom, but in my frazzled state,

I wanted to talk through the things racing through my mind with someone I trusted.

And though the first person who popped into my head surprised me, I didn't think twice about the direction my feet led me.

Each step forward was weighed down by the information circling my head, and as I stepped outside, there was a part of me that wanted to march out towards the forest to uncover the hideaway once again. To look for more of the missing pieces of the puzzle.

But I knew that now wasn't the time.

Instead, I kept my focus, ignoring the chill that the night air held, and made my way across the grass to the training barn.

Despite the sun having set, there were still a few hours left in the training day – which meant that as I slipped inside the barn, I was greeted with the sight and sounds of several agents working on their combat skills. Casting my gaze around the room, it didn't take me long to find who I was looking for amidst the small crowd.

"Beckett."

After a final punch to the bag in front of him, he stepped back and turned my way. "Aspen," he started, though his features pinched with concern when he noticed the uneasiness clouding my features. "What is it?" he asked, his voice deepening as he moved towards me. "What's wrong?"

"Can we talk?" I asked, a frantic feeling of urgency bubbling in the pit of my stomach as I lowered my voice to a whisper. "Somewhere private?"

If he was thrown by my request, he hid it well. There was no sign of hesitation on his end as he nodded with immediate agreement, reaching for my free hand with his own before guiding me back out of the barn. Having not missed a beat, his hands were still fitted in a well-worn pair of training gloves, the material causing friction against my palm before he slipped his hand free when we came up on the nearest entrance to the main building.

The corridor was empty, and though our movements were on the verge of urgent, neither of us wanted to pull in unnecessary attention. The tension in the air was thick – a burden that we both carried in silence as we reached the stairs and began climbing.

"Are you okay?" Beckett asked under his breath, turning to glance my way as we reached the hall where his room was. My steps slowed as I met his gaze, watching as he scanned over my features, trying to find a clue as to what was going on.

"I'm fine," I insisted, averting my gaze.

We reached his room several seconds later, at which time he produced a small key from his pocket. As he slipped it into the lock, I looked back over my shoulder. The hallway was dead, and this was about as private as a place we were going to find at this hour to talk.

Once inside, I moved further into the room while Beckett shut the door behind us, flipping the lock to make sure we weren't interrupted.

Hovering near the door, he stayed silent, waiting for me to make the first move and start talking. The problem was,

I didn't know where to start. I let myself sink down on the end of his bed, going over everything quickly in my head, but I didn't realize that I'd subconsciously been running my fingers over the symbol on the back of the book that I still held tightly in my hand.

"What do you have there?" Beckett asked, his voice pulling me back to the situation at hand. Taking a seat beside me, his hand came down over mine to grab a closer look before narrowing his eyes. "Aspen... why have you been reading up on the Gemini Clan?"

"Because I wanted answers," I replied firmly. "Nothing was adding up, and since nobody would give me the information I wanted – "

"They didn't need to, Aspen," Beckett stressed. "It's not your job to solve every piece of the puzzle. In fact, your only real role in all of this is to stay safe and let everyone else do the hard work. You might think that because it's your father who's spearheading the Gemini Clan right now – "

"Don't call him that," I cut in forcefully.

He paused for a moment, a flicker of understanding crossing his features. "Sorry," he said before continuing. "But Aspen, there are agents who've been training for years – people who know the risks they're taking, and they're the ones who are standing guard 24/7 and being sent out to take down the Gemini Clan. That's their job, not yours."

I let my gaze fall to my lap, knowing he was right but wanting to prove him wrong. "There's someone on the inside though," I said quietly. "Someone who's taking advantage of their position to help the Gemini Clan."

It wasn't a question, but a statement. One that Beckett regretfully agreed with. "It's possible, yes."

"And if they're working from inside the Division, don't you think they know the obstacles? They know where the cameras and the guards are. They'll find a way to get things done without being noticed." He gave no response as I paused, exhaling slowly. "This symbol," I started, drawing his attention back to the book that rested in my hands, "you've seen it before."

Knowing that he'd recognized it as something to do with the Gemini Clan, it wasn't a surprise when he nodded. "It was Division 13's marking before they were cut off from S.I.C.O," he replied. "Each Division has one, but I've only ever seen them used on official reports and documentation."

"Do you know if they were ever used for other purposes?"

His forehead creased. "Like what?"

"Say... to mark a Division's territory?"

The curiosity that filled his features shifted quickly to wariness. "Aspen," Beckett started cautiously, as if bracing himself for what was to come, "what are you trying to say?"

It was then that my nerves came to fruition, though that didn't stop me from finally freeing every thought inside my head. "Just beyond the grounds, a few feet into the trees, I found this entrance to an underground hideaway. I don't know if the senior agents know about it, or if it's something that was supposed to stay a secret, but there were files down there. There was an old computer and shelves of books, but up until an hour ago, I hadn't considered the possibility that the space might not belong to Division 27." I smoothed my hand over the symbol once more. "This symbol... it was etched into the concrete entrance."

I wasn't sure if this was something Beckett had already been aware of, but as I peeked up from my lap to see his expressionless face, I considered the possibility that he'd been almost as in the dark as I'd been.

"When was this?" he asked calmly, though I suspected it was taking everything he had to contain his emotions.

"Almost two weeks ago," I replied. "That night I stayed out after training."

Expecting a lecture on the dangers of what I'd done, I braced myself. But it never came.

"I'll talk to Catherine to see if she knows anything about it," he said instead. "It's possible it's just an old hideaway that was forgotten over the years. Or that the symbol was put there ages ago by someone trying to make a joke."

The first option was plausible, but the latter choice was a reach, making it sound as though he was trying to convince himself that this was nothing more than a coincidence.

As he went to stand up, thinking that I'd revealed all I'd meant to, I placed a hand on his arm to stop him. "Wait," I said gravely. "That's not all."

He lifted his hand to his hair, running his fingers through it in a frustrated motion as my hand fell back to my lap. "What more is there?"

"That night... I wasn't alone in the hideaway. Finn was down there." I stayed quiet for a moment, letting my words sink in. "He claimed he was down there looking for something to use against the Gemini Clan. That the room was an old records room that S.I.C.O had abandoned, but before I could see what he was doing, he said he had to be up early and it was best we both head up to bed. Now I don't know what he was really doing down there, but it didn't look all that innocent, no matter how he tried to make it seem. He's hiding something, and even though I can't say for sure if he's the one who's been betraying the Division to assist the Gemini Clan – " I took a deep breath. " – I think you were right about him. About the fact that he can't be trusted."

I expected some kind of reaction from Beckett – a curse, anger, an I told you so. Something. Instead, I was met with a void of silence that dragged on painstakingly long, only to be broken as the beginnings of a tremor began to make its way through my body.

"I'll do my best to find out what's going on," Beckett said, shocking me as he kept his anger inside and tipped my chin up so that my gaze met his, "but you have to promise me something."

"Anything."

"Do not try to confront Finn. If he really has turned his back on this Division, being around him isn't safe. Not for anyone."

His eyes were dark, his tone firm, and as I nodded my head, I wished more than anything that I could figure out what was currently running through his head. "I promise," I replied quietly, trying to ignore the unsettling feeling that ignited in my chest that told me the words were likely a lie.

Chapter 18

I was at a loss for words.

Standing beside Kira just a few days later, I watched as she rested one of her hands on the lab bench in front of us, using her other to place a small piece of cloth on top of it. It took a few seconds, but right before my eyes I saw her hand disappear. I blinked, making sure it wasn't just my imagination, but when nothing changed, a laugh of wonder escaped my lips.

"It's – "

When I paused, trying to come up with the right word, Kira turned towards me with a wide grin. "Pretty cool, right?" Her excitement was contagious as she deposited the material back alongside the rest of the prototypes. "I still need to tweak the formulation a bit to make sure that larger pieces of material can work the way I need them to without any complications, but I think I'm almost there."

I shook my head in amazement. "Seriously, this is incredible," I said, running my fingers over the fabric in front of me. If I didn't know any better, I'd think it was just an everyday piece of material – nothing special about it. "I didn't even think this type of technology existed."

"You've probably said that about more than a few things since you got here," she mused.

And she was right.

Never in a million years did I think I'd be where I was today. Just two months ago I'd been waitressing full-time, working extra shifts to save up enough money for the possibility of attending university. Fast forward and now I'd witnessed technological breakthroughs, trained with some of the best agents in the world, and had fallen deep into the world of covert operations.

"Seems that way," I replied. Glancing around the room I noticed that, while we were the only two currently occupying the lab, almost every lab bench had bits and pieces strewn across it. "Is this all yours?"

"Most of it," Kira replied, hopping down off her stool before moving around to do a bit of a cleanup. I stayed where I was, not wanting to risk accidentally ruining something that was important. "Catherine's been pushing a lot of other high-level security projects in motion the last couple of days, and with the veteran lab technicians handling those, I'm more or less on my own with the trials I have to run."

"If you need help, I can always pitch in," I offered. "I may not know a whole lot about all of this," I continued, waving my hands around the room to signal the various lab equipment, "but I can do some of the grunt work. Writing down observations, data collection... that sort of thing."

The corners of her lips pulled upwards as she piled a few wires and a small machine into her arms, carrying them back over to the bench I stood beside. "Thanks," she said, "but I think I'll be okay. If, for some reason though, things change, I'll let you know."

I nodded in understanding. "So... what's – "

The words dried up on my lips as the beeping of the lab door captured my attention, and I inhaled sharply as I realized the newcomer was Finn.

Having taken Beckett's advice two nights ago, I hadn't sought him out, and this was the first time, besides the odd passing in the Grand Hall, that I was really seeing him since that evening in the hideaway. My first instinct was to allow my anger to get the best of me – to march over to him and hound him until he told me why he was helping a Division whose building blocks took the form of malice and revenge.

But that wouldn't be smart.

Instead, I stood still. Staying quiet and taking small, calming breaths, my eyes tracked each movement that Finn made as he greeted Kira with a smile and nodded towards the cabinets that kept the field gadgets locked up.

"Is there enough for me to stock up for tonight?" he asked.

Kira nodded, though followed closely behind him. "I'll have to let you in though. I had to change the code last night."

"What, you don't trust me?" he asked teasingly.

She shouldn't. The thought rushed to the forefront of my mind, but I managed to reel it back before the words slipped out.

"It's not that," she started to explain, "but I'm airing on the side of caution for the next couple of days." She unlocked the door to the cabinet, pulling it open. "I came down to check on some things last night only to find out that the feed on the security cameras had been cut and the lock on the lab door had been disabled."

"What?" I asked sharply, as it was the first time I was hearing this.

Kira sent a sheepish look of apology in my direction, but turned back towards Finn as he asked if she'd reported it. A frown tugged at his lips – a seemingly genuine worry taking hold of him.

Though I didn't buy it.

"Of course I did," she replied, waving at him to take what he needed. As Finn began to peruse the gadget cabinet and load his belt, she continued. "I was up half the night with some of the other lab technicians and senior agents scouring the place for any sign of intrusion, but we couldn't find anything. Whatever happened last night, nothing was tampered with or stolen."

"Just be careful, alright?" he replied, stepping back so that she could lock up the cabinet and jot down all he'd taken.

Finn didn't deserve the grateful smile he got in return. "You too – on your assignment, tonight."

"I won't need it," he grinned, winking at her and causing her to shake her head in amusement as he turned on his heel.

While he left without so much as a glance in my direction, my gaze stayed glued to his back right up until the moment the lab door closed behind him – which didn't go unnoticed by Kira.

"So..." She quirked an eyebrow. "Are you going to tell me what's going on between the two of you?"

I hadn't told her about my suspicions of Finn. I hadn't told anybody except Beckett, and even though he'd said he would look into it, I wasn't privy to what that truly meant. But as I brought my attention back around to Kira, a sinking feeling in the pit of my stomach told me that keeping the information inside had been the wrong way to go.

"Does it have something to do with Beckett?" she pressed when I didn't respond right away. "I know you guys are growing closer, what with training and everything, but did Finn find out? Is that why he's giving you the cold shoulder?"

I shook my head, wishing the problem could be that simple.

"Then what?"

"Um... how good are you at keeping secrets, even if it might not be the best thing to do?"

She quirked an eyebrow. "You do realize you're talking to someone who has been a part of a central intelligence organization for the past four years, right?"

"Right," I said, a sad attempt at a laugh slipping through. "Well, it's just, I don't think we can trust Finn."

"Excuse me?" I flinched backwards at her disbelief. It took her a moment to fully process what I'd said, her eyes growing wide with astonishment. "Aspen, what makes you think that?" she asked, her voice quiet and filled with dread.

"Well," I started hesitantly before recounting the events that backed up my claim. The behaviour that had me questioning him. The underground hideaway and the possibility of its contents belonging to Division 13. The symbol. It was almost exactly what I'd told Beckett, except this time I was able to get straight to the point. "Plus, I get the feeling that the upbeat persona he holds is just a façade," I added on. "If he is working against us, it would've been beneficial for him to gain the trust of everyone here first, and I can't think of a better way to do that than by playing the part of an ambitious and good-hearted agent."

As I trailed off, Kira pursed her lips. "So, you think Finn is a double agent?"

"Like I said, I'm not one hundred percent sure," I replied, "but yeah, I do."

It was then that her shoulders deflated, as though the secondary confirmation was all that she needed to secure the idea in her head. Deep breaths were taken as the silence was drawn out, but when her gaze aligned with mine once more, she was looking to me for guidance. "Well, what do we do now?"

"I don't know," I said gravely, "not yet, anyways."

That night I tossed and turned, barely getting a wink of sleep. My mind just wouldn't shut down, and after Kira's reaction, the guilt in my chest grew by the minute, wondering if I'd only caused more harm than good by keeping my suspicions about Finn to myself.

When the sun began to peak above the skyline, I rolled out of bed, but instead of feeling drowsy, I felt empowered. During the night, as I stared endlessly at my ceiling, and willed some kind of plan to take shape, I'd resigned myself to the fact that, whether there was weight behind my accusations or not, Catherine needed to know about Finn.

I didn't expect her to believe me right away, but if I could at least get her and a few of the other senior agents to keep a close watch over him, then I'd consider it a win.

After splashing my face with water and brushing my teeth, I changed out of the clothes I'd worn to bed and pulled on my shoes before slipping out the door. The halls were quiet at the early hour, though I did pass by a few agents returning from an overnight assignment – the exhaustion on their faces and scuff marks on their clothes evidence of their hard work.

However, just as I started up the stairs that led towards Catherine's office, I stopped short and was forced to move to the side. A woman a few years older than myself – an agent I'd never spoken to before but had seen around the Division – came rushing down the slim staircase. Her fire red hair was pulled back in a wild ponytail, and though I wondered how she managed to be discrete with her vibrant mane, that wasn't what caught my attention.

No. What caught my attention was the look of anguish sketched into her features. Bloodshot eyes, tears staining her cheeks, and pinched lips to contain the wails of despair that threatened to escape.

She paid me no attention as she rushed passed, and though she disappeared a second later, the sound of her rushed footsteps continued to echo off the stone as the air around me grew thick with an overwhelming sense of dread.

When I reached the top of the staircase, the only door that stood slightly ajar was Catherine's. There were two voices, and though the scene flashed me back to the last time I'd stepped foot in her office – when I'd come face to face with Damon – this time I breathed slightly easier knowing that I recognized who they belonged to.

I took a few steps forward, trying not to give myself away as I moved to listen in. Before I could get close enough to hear anything more than hushed whispers however, their conversation was abruptly cut off and the door to Catherine's office was pulled all the way open.

Immediately taken aback by the mixture of melancholy and anger that painted their features, I felt the colour drain from my face. "What is it?" I asked desperately. "What's happened?"

Indecision crossed both of their faces, but after a drawn-out silence in which they both looked to each other for support, Joe was the one who turned to me with a reply. "There's been an accident."

My breath hitched. "What... who...?" I stuttered, unable to form a coherent sentence. My mind suddenly went to the worst-case scenario, causing my hands to shake and my eyes to widen with fear. "Beckett? Kira? Are they...?"

"They're fine," Joe was quick to reassure as Catherine stepped aside, ushering me into the office. I barely felt the small weight lift from my chest at the knowledge my friends were safe. The worry was still there, all-consuming, as I waited to hear what had happened. "One of our recent assignments succeeded when a group of agents came back with a lead – a clue as to what the Gemini Clan had planned to do next."

"Last night," Catherine took over, a somber tone to her voice, "we sent out two agents to follow that lead and report back with anything they found, but unfortunately, things didn't go according to plan." She shut her eyes for a moment, her chest expanding as she inhaled deeply before continuing. "From what we know, one of the agents – Sean, didn't make it out alive."

A jolt went through me, feeling as though a knife had been dug straight into my heart. Sean had been an experienced agent, and though I'd never spoken to him, it wasn't as though I'd never seen him around. I could remember glimpses of him training in the barn and relaxing in the Grand Hall after a rough day. He fit in effortlessly, and even as an onlooker, there was no question as to whether he belonged within these walls.

And now he was dead.

"And the other agent?" I asked, my voice thick with emotion, wondering if I even wanted to know the answer. "What happened to them?"

"We have reason to believe that they were able to make it out alive, but they've gone off the grid. Without knowing the extent of any injuries, we can't be sure of anything right now."

"So, they're just missing?" I asked, and when I received a nod in response, my brows drew tight with confusion. Surely the Division had ways of finding out where a missing agent was located, either by tracking them down or getting word of their whereabouts. "Who is it?"

Catherine gaze shifted to one of sympathy. "Finn."

The sound of his name made my blood run cold. "F-Finn?" I clarified, my posture stiff as my gaze darted between her and Joe. "Finn Westin?"

"I know you two were friends," she said solemnly, "but – "

I cut off her warning before she could give it, shaking my head venomously. "No, you don't understand. I came up here to warn you – I think Finn's the one that's been helping the Gemini Clan."

The surprise on their faces was immediate, my revelation clearly not what they'd been expecting.

"Aspen, that's a serious accusation," Joe said, masking his emotions as he approached the conversation with caution. "Do you have any proof?"

"It's not concrete," I swallowed, "but ever since I caught him down in one of the hideaways just beyond the trees – one with Division 13's symbol etched into the entrance, he's been careful with his efforts to avoid me."

At the mention of the underground hideaway, the frown on Catherine's face deepened. "I'm aware of the hideaway," she responded when I brought it up, questioning its purpose, "but to my knowledge, because of its connection to the Gemini Clan, it was sealed up years ago."

This, of course, did nothing to calm the uneasiness in my stomach.

I went on, explaining the night that I'd found him, what he was doing, the suspicions I had, and everything else that, in my mind, incriminated him as a trader.

As they digested all that I was saying, I had a front row seat to watch their reactions. It was clear they were trying to appear undeterred, but they weren't quick enough to mask the lightning fast appearances of fear, wariness, and shock that flitted across their features.

"If what you're saying is true," Catherine began apprehensively, "then it may be safe to assume that last night's assignment was compromised."

I blinked at her, because in my frazzled state, I'd somehow skipped over that possibility.

Finn wasn't missing. The lead that had directed them into the Gemini Clan's clutches was likely a planned trap, set up to allow Finn a way to defect from Division 27 without suggesting he'd betrayed them. And Sean's death hadn't been an accident – it'd been a necessary part of Finn's agenda.

I could tell that Catherine and Joe were no longer concerned with what was going on in this room, or even within this Division. While I was still trying to understand everything that had transpired, their minds were several steps ahead, figuring out strategies on how to protect the loyal agents of this Division, as well as what tactics they'd need to implement moving forward.

"Alert S.I.C.O," Catherine instructed, turning to face Joe. "If the Gemini Clan is getting ready to attack, then we need all the help we can get to make sure we're ready for a fight."

Chapter 19

For some reason, I'd assumed that the Gemini Clan would hold off on their attack. That they'd lure us into a false sense of security until our worries began to diminish, waiting until there was a sliver of vulnerability in our defenses to strike.

Only that didn't happen.

Once the news of Finn's betrayal spread, it was as though everyone within the Division was suddenly on edge. There were whispers everywhere – wondering whether he was the only traitor amongst the Division's ranks and, if one of the best could be lured in by the Gemini Clan, what was stopping other agents from jumping ship as well.

It didn't get any better when, later that night, Joe rounded up a small team of senior agents to scope out the underground hideaway. Situated in just the right spot, the hideaway was hidden behind too many trees for any camera to have a clear shot of it, and seeing as it was still within the grounds line, it was discovered that no alarm would sound if someone were to infiltrate the space.

Clearly Finn, or whoever had last used the space, had sought to cover their tracks. The hideaway was completely destroyed. Books which had once sat untouched on ancient shelves were knocked to the ground and torched, their ashes all that remained. The rest of the space had been ransacked, leaving a giant hole in the computer screen and significant physical damage to the hard drive, making it clear that the person responsible had made damn sure that there was nothing left over for us to find.

In the days that followed, Catherine essentially ordered the Division into lockdown. Everyone – whether they were senior agents or trainees – was made aware of what was going on. Security was tightened and, due to the assistance of S.I.C.O, experienced agents were transferred to our grounds each day.

And though the conversations about the weapon within our walls was kept relatively quiet, I had picked up enough to know that S.I.C.O had considered moving it before the Gemini Clan could get their hands on it. Whether it was transferred or kept as is, there were pros and cons, but in the end, the decision to keep the weapon where it was prevailed.

No one wanted to risk moving the weapon and, consequently, give the Gemini Clan an easier target.

Furthermore, outgoing assignments quickly transitioned into an oddity – kept on hold in the interest of safety, and with nearly every agent sticking close to the Division, it made for a restless environment. There were daily meetings held in the Grand Hall in which possible defensive strategies were plotted and mapped out for a wide possibility of attacks.

Sure, we had a plan. One in which everyone had a role, but even the best made plans had the potential for failure.

And suddenly, sooner than expected, the day of reckoning descended upon us.

It was a Monday morning, five days after Finn's disappearance, and alongside numerous other agents, I'd been in the Grand Hall when the alarms began to sound. The moment everyone had subconsciously been waiting for.

The senior agents jumped into action immediately, with the junior agents not far behind. They'd been out in the field before – had experienced the nature of real-world combat, and with their weapons at the ready, they all began to move to their assigned positions. The trainees however, including myself, were a little slower on the pick-up.

It didn't matter that we were all on light duty – helping secure the building and acting as a second line of defense, or that we'd attended lessons and learned from the best. Nothing could truly prepare us for the fight to come.

Nevertheless, once the hesitation began to fade and our fears were pushed aside, we abandoned the feeling of security the Grand Hall offered and got to work.

I took a detour however, since everyone but me, it seemed, had come prepared.

Climbing the stairs in a rush, I reached my room and pushed open the door in record time. I dropped to the floor just a few feet from the bed, reaching underneath until I found the gadgets Kira had given me to use for protection. There was a small pouch of smoke beads – which produced thick clouds of black smoke when set off, a pair of night vision goggles, two vials of healing solution, a bracelet that acted as a lock decoder, and a stun gun. The latter was capable of blasting an enemy backwards while a rush of electrical energy kept them incapacitated for a short period of time, and though its power terrified me slightly, having it strapped to my waist also gave me an extra layer of protection.

With my gaze drawn to the window as I stood, I froze momentarily. Down below, the grounds were filled with agents of the Gemini Clan, and while the numbers appeared to be tilted in our favour, the margin was small. This wasn't surprising. They were invading, and if they wanted to be successful, they'd need more than just a few agents.

My eyes quickly searched the chaos for Finn and Damon, wondering where they'd be positioned in the attack, but when I failed to locate them, a red alert went off in my head.

Of course.

They weren't out there because the fight was just a distraction. The real mission was to secure the weapon hidden within the depths of the building before making a quick getaway. My eyes grew wide at the startling realization. Finn knew these grounds like the back of his hand, and Damon had gotten into the building once before, so if they had figured out the exact spot the weapon was hidden, what was stopping them from going around our defenses to grab it and run?

There was a flicker of indecision as a plan began to form – one that strayed from the instructions I'd been given. It wasn't smart. It wasn't logical. It was dangerous, especially considering I didn't know exactly where the weapon was hidden in the first place.

But I had a guess, and in that moment, it was enough to ignite a fire in my chest and push me forward.

Since most of the action was being contained to the outer grounds, the halls were left relatively empty. Every person I passed was deep in their element – whether that was preparing for a fight or standing guard, and in their preoccupied state, no one thought to pay me a second glance.

Keeping my eyes forward, I didn't dare glance back, worried that if I did, the reality of the situation would consume me. That I was going against everyone I'd come to know here, essentially letting them all down, just to prove to myself that I could step up. That I could handle myself in the field and do what needed to be done in the name of protection.

I was forging my own way.

It was only when I rounded a corner to see Beckett fighting off not one, but two men, that my steps came to a staggering halt. I watched, frozen, as he landed a punch to the stomach of one man, only to turn around a send a round-house kick to the other's jaw. My eyes grew wide before flashing with recognition, noticing that both of his opponents had been there the night I'd been attacked.

One being the man who'd tried his best to follow me home.

There was a brief pang in my chest as I thought back to my old life, but the scene inside my mind was quickly cut off when I saw Beckett flinch backwards after a punch to the jaw.

A horrified gasp left my lips, watching as the other man readied himself for an attack of his own, and before I could stop myself, I screeched his name with horror. "Beckett!"

Beckett didn't glance my way, but at the sound of his name, something clicked inside of him. Before the second man could land another hard shot to his face, Beckett dodged his fist and retaliated. Two punches and a knee to the stomach had the man sprawling to the ground, and if that wasn't enough, Beckett bent over the man, gripping the material of his t-shirt to pull his body off the ground and swung his other fist aggressively into his nose, knocking him unconscious.

Without missing a beat, one of Beckett's legs swung backwards to trip his other opponent up. In the sequence of targeted attacks that followed – a nudge, a few kicks, and two square punches to the face, it was evident that Beckett had the upper hand.

When the threat had been neutralized, I couldn't stop myself from moving towards Beckett, closing the distance between us. "Are you okay?" I asked, my eyes scanning his features with worry.

His bottom lip was split and the hit he'd taken to the jaw would surely leave a mark, but other than looking a bit out of sorts, he seemed okay. "I'm fine, Aspen," he confirmed, "but I need to get back out there."

He was right, but as he went to step away, I stopped him. Pushing myself up on my tiptoes, I brushed my lips against his. I tried to be gentle as I felt him freeze at the contact, but even the smallest amount of pressure caused him to hiss, so I pulled back.

"Sorry." There was a brief flash of admiration in his eyes, though it was mixed with shock, and if I didn't have my mind set on putting an end to the chaos we were currently in, I would've brought his head back down to kiss him again. But I knew better. "I'll see you later."

My words were a promise, one that meant I had faith we'd both make it out of this insanity, and his lips pulled upwards in a genuine smile. "Go," he said, "I've got this handled."

An ounce of guilt shot through me, knowing that he believed I was heading to safety when he was actually pushing me towards danger. And while I felt the truth crawling to the surface, I couldn't tell him my plan – he'd only try and stop me.

Instead I nodded, flashing him a fake grin before I turned on my heel and made my getaway.

Brought back to the events of the last alarm when I'd shadowed Catherine through unknown corridors, I tried to retrace our steps. There was something odd about that dead-end hallway we'd ended up in, and I had a sneaking suspicion that when Catherine had up and disappeared, she'd merely slipped into a hidden passageway unnoticed.

And if I could find that passageway, I was willing to bet it'd lead to the weapon's hiding spot.

The guards along the way however, posed a problem. They were stationed in groups to stop Gemini agents from infiltrating deep into the building, but they'd also been ordered to keep out any wandering agents from our side as well. Just to be safe.

Standing tall and acting as though I belonged, I made a split-second decision to use who I was as an advantage. After all, I wasn't the threat they needed to be concerned about.

"Catherine wants to know if there's been any hint of movement," I'd say to the guards, not above dropping her name to suit my needs. Stopping to check with each security group I passed, I waited as they explained that everything was clear. Nobody had been down here yet. After each encounter, I'd nod and thank them for their cooperation before moving on, getting closer to the dead-end hallway every minute.

When I reached the last group of guards, I knew that moving passed them would cause a spark of interest. What was I doing? Where did I think I was going? Why wasn't I out helping the other trainees?

I wasn't naïve enough to think they'd not been told about the weapon they were guarding – that they were the absolute last physical line of defense, but I wasn't convinced that, if there was a passageway hidden around the corner, they'd know how to get to it. So, I just had to find it before they caught me.

One of the guards tilted his head, his gaze narrowing after I'd gone through my spiel and failed to leave. "Aspen, shouldn't you be reporting back to Catherine?"

My palms began to sweat, wondering what would happen if this didn't work. "I just have to check..." I trailed off, pointing around the corner as I slipped passed them and around the corner.

There had to be something here.

Behind me, the uproar was immediate. My steps quickened as a result, and I didn't stop until my hands hit the walls of the dead-end hallway. I was surrounded with nowhere to go.

"Aspen! Hey," one guard yelled forcefully, anger shadowing his words. "Stop, now!"

"Shit," I winced, looking over my shoulder to see that while some of the guards had stayed back, three were hot on my heels. Turning away from them, I tapped desperately and repeatedly on the wall in different spots, hoping that some kind of secret passage would appear.

But I had no such luck.

Thinking quickly, my fingers skimmed my belt for the smoke beads, knowing they'd be the most effective. Grabbing a handful, I threw them to the ground and in an instant, a wall of hazy black smoke filled the hall.

The abrupt loss of their surroundings caused surprised gasps to fill the air.

Ducking to the ground, I held my breath, pressing my hands against the wall to guide myself. I knew that even if I circled back and escaped, I would face the rest of the guards, so the only way I could get out was by moving forward.

In hopes that I'd bought myself a few seconds while the guards were discombobulated, I continued my search for some kind of passageway. It was difficult, considering I couldn't distinguish which direction I was facing or what exactly I was doing, but when a stone beneath my palm suddenly gave way, I was too shocked for my accomplishment to sink in.

Tumbling forwards as a section of the wall swung open, my knees were the first to hit the ground, followed by my hands. Barely a second passed before I heard the low thud of the entrance closing behind me, keeping out the smoke but immersing me in total darkness.

As I stumbled to my feet, I realized that besides the echoes of my movements, the place was silent – the stone blocking out all remnants of chaos beyond the tunnel walls.

I patted my belt, feeling around for the night vision goggles I was thankful to have in that moment. Unclipping them, I pulled them on and breathed easier as my surroundings came into view, albeit tinged green though the lenses.

Turning back to the wall I'd fallen through, there was no evidence of a door. Just like the hall on the other side, it appeared to be nothing more than a dead-end. But now I knew that there was a door, a passageway, that could only be opened by a fair few who knew what they were looking for.

The only problem was that I had no idea what I'd done to gain access, and no clue if there was another way out. But those thoughts took an immediate back seat to my goal – to find the weapon that was surely hidden somewhere along this corridor, and guarantee its protection.

Moving slowly through the passageway, my eyes never stopped moving. I scanned every crevice in the stones, will-ing a clue to appear yet coming up with nothing. It wasn't until I hit a small alcove, which gave way to a downwards staircase, that I felt the small burst of optimism sink in.

This had to be it.

Moving deeper underground, I kept my hands firm on the stone walls – a necessary precaution as I felt the moisture in the air increasing. The steps were slippery beneath my boots, and one wrong move would no doubt send me sprawling down who knows how many steps.

It was minutes later when the stairs finally came to an end, giving way to a small circular room. There were six beaten down iron doors that surrounded the exterior, the spaces they blocked looking as though they'd been used to house prisoners back in the day, though I didn't pay them much attention.

My gaze was drawn to the opposite side of the room, between two of the doors, where a small dagger rested atop a protruded stone.

Disbelief coursed through me. This was what the Gemini Clan were searching for – the reason behind their attack? I'd envisioned a nuclear grenade or a scientifically enhanced gun, but this? This dagger looked like one you'd find in a medieval video game, carved extensively and stretching no longer than my forearm.

Suddenly I found myself moving across the room, wanting to know what about this weapon warranted the amount of secrecy and precaution that it'd brought up.

However, as I reached out to touch it, I froze right before my hand came in contact with the carved steel. Rooted to the spot, I heard footsteps echoing down the stairs I'd just descended from. When they slowed however, I gulped, turning my head to meet the gaze of the intruder.

"I wouldn't do that if I were you."

Chapter 20

Finn.

Despite the way my spine locked and shoulders tensed, I was able to keep my breathing calm and my features blank as I turned fully to face him, blocking the dagger from his line of sight.

Compared to the person who had once appeared to be the embodiment of a faithful agent – the golden boy of Division 27 – it was startling to see the man standing in front of me looking severely worse for wear. His eyes, having previously gleamed with joy and a hint of mischief, now appeared to be dark pools of resentment. There were tight lines forming around his mouth, making it seem like he hadn't cracked a smile since he'd left, and his smooth complexion had been tarnished with bruises and fading cuts, presumably from the night he'd escaped.

"Well you don't look surprised," he all but snarled. "But then again," he clicked his tongue, "you're the one who forced me to leave, so why would you?"

He had the audacity to blame this all on me? I raised an eyebrow in disbelief. "You think this is my fault?"

"Call it a hunch, but considering I saw Beckett snooping around passed the tree line about a week ago, I think you just couldn't keep your mouth shut about that hideaway." A manic smirk pulled at his lips. "Not that there was anything left for you all to find."

"And you thought that would help your cover?" I asked, holding back a dry laugh at his disillusions. "Because newsflash, it just put the final nail in your coffin. Catherine, Joe, the other agents... everyone knows you're a traitor, and I highly doubt there's a chance of you getting out of here tonight scot-free."

"Oh? And who's going to stop me... you?"

Thinly veiled amusement flashed across his eyes, as if it was unthinkable for me – a woman trainee without a substantial amount of experience – to take on the likes of him. And while it may be a stretch, this wasn't all about strength. I had other methods at my disposal.

All I needed to do was keep him talking, prolonging his attempt at capturing the dagger.

Ignoring his previous comment, I quirked an eyebrow and crossed my arms across my chest, displaying a fabricated confidence. "Shouldn't it have been Damon down here, wanting the glory of stealing the dagger for himself?"

There was a brief moment where the twisted pleasure fell from his face, only to appear once again. His grin was wide and wicked. "He didn't want to miss out on all the fun to be had above ground," he replied. "More so, he wanted to deal with your mother... directly."

A lump formed in my throat, and I could feel the sinking feeling expanding deep within my chest, but I shook it off. I knew full well that Catherine could hold her own.

"So, he sent you to do the dirty work?" I asked, pushing him for some kind of information. "Are you just another one of his puppets then?"

In an instant, his eyes darkened and his fists clenched at his sides. "You don't know what you're talking about," he said, trying to contain the anger that bubbled inside him.

"Don't I?" I challenged, pausing only for a moment before pressing on. "I know that someone managed to convince you to jump sides, and if it wasn't Damon, who was it?" His anger became more pronounced the longer I spoke. "I mean, after growing up in this Division, after hearing all the rumours and stories about the Gemini Clan, how did you ever think that joining them would end well?"

It was a valid question – one I wanted to hear his honest answer for, despite knowing this conversation was nothing more than a ploy to deter his mind from the real reason he was here.

"Everyone is so quick to believe that the Gemini Clan is the worst of the worst," he started, "but that's because they don't want to see the truth. S.I.C.O was formed to go beyond the capabilities of government run central intelligence agencies – to be ruthless and cunning when the situation called for it. They needed agents that would do anything to get the job done, and that's exactly what the Gemini Clan does."

"S.I.C.O was built to operate outside of the government, yes, but they still fight for justice. They still take precautions when it comes to getting the job done," I countered. "The Gemini Clan doesn't operate under that guise. They're reckless and have been overrun with greed. All they're after is power."

"And how could you possibly know this?" Finn scoffed. "You been here, what, two months? You don't even know a fraction of what's gone on through the years that S.I.C.O's been involved in. The Gemini Clan is no worse."

I was taken aback by his response. How could he say that? In just the short time I'd been here, I'd read the reports and heard stories all about what the Gemini Clan had done, both in the past and the present, and none of it had been good.

Yes, S.I.C.O and the Divisions beneath it had killed and imprisoned people – bad people. Criminals. Where the Gemini Clan was concerned however, the innocent could be used as a means to an end. They didn't care. And considering I'd almost been one of their chess pieces on the night of my birthday, I knew this first-hand.

My mouth opened, closed, and then opened again before the words I was searching for finally formed on my tongue. "They've killed innocent people, Finn!"

"And so has S.I.C.O!" he replied, his words echoing loudly off the stone walls. I felt the colour drain from my face. "What?" A sinister laugh left his lips. "Did you think S.I.C. O was above killing the innocent, or better yet, their own agents?"

It couldn't be true.

This Division. S.I.C.O. They'd helped protect me. They'd done so much over the years, all of which was documented, but even though I knew in my gut what he was saying held no weight, the possibility of his words being even the tiniest bit true placed a small drop of doubt in my mind.

"And where's your proof?" I asked, my voice remaining steady.

"Proof?" Finn clenched his teeth as he spat out the word. "You want proof? How about going back to the night my parents left on an assignment and never came back? My life was fine, my family was happy, and then the Division had to go and send both my parents out on a suicide mission. They were supposed to be investigating a known hangout for the masterminds behind an underground drug ring, but they barely made it through the door before they were blown to smithereens." I saw the flash of misery that crossed his features before he could mask it. "The Division thought they could cover up the truth about that night, but Damon made sure I knew how it really went down."

Sympathy flooded my mind as he spoke, right up until his last statement, and then it was replaced with pity as things slowly began to add up.

"My parents had overheard classified plans for another mission just days before – one they weren't a part of," Finn continued, equal parts frustrated, angry, and hurt. "A rogue agent that they'd previously partnered with had fallen deep into trouble playing by his own rules, and S.I.C.O was gearing up to bring him in. When they caught wind that my parents were also privy to this information, the Division got worried, and thinking that they'd betray them, sent them on a mission that was meant for their demise."

While I didn't doubt the fact that his parents had died that night when they been sent out on an assignment, it was highly unlikely that it had been set up as a death trap. His parents had known the risks and had accepted them, just as Finn did every time he was sent out.

"Finn..." I trailed softly, "why did you take Damon's word for it? He's the leader of the Gemini Clan. It's highly likely that he could spin together a few loose ends and lie – "

"He wasn't," he roared adamantly, causing me to flinch backwards. "He had proof... things lined up..."

I stared at him, watching as he went still and hoped with every fiber in my being that he was coming to see the light. Seeing that he'd been played. That Damon had found the perfect way to manipulate him – by twisting the truth and flipping the picture of the weakest link in Finn's past.

But as the seconds drew on, I realized he wasn't recogniz-ing his wrongs at all, but staring right past me, his eyes locked on the dagger.

Without meaning to, I'd mistakenly shifted a step to the right, putting the dagger that rested behind me right into Finn's line of sight.

A moment passed, and then another before he spoke.

"It doesn't look like much, does it?" he asked, his tone much more subdued. He didn't glance at me once, his eyes unwa-vering from the steel. "Just a small dagger fit for a beginner in the field." He paused. "But that's what makes it so powerful."

I tore my gaze away from him for just a moment as I glanced over my shoulder at the dagger, noting that while the steel was carved beautifully – with lines that weaved their own pattern etched intricately onto the surface, he was right. It didn't appear to be worthy of these high levels of protection.

"When S.I.C.O was experimenting with new ways to gain a leg up on their enemies back in the day, they created this dagger," he said. "It's said that when the steel was forged, a poison was mixed into the molten metal – one that was all-consuming. Just one touch of the blade could cause your skin to burn, and if the blade was to pierce your skin, you'd be dead before you felt it."

My eyes widened at the information, part of me grateful that he'd stopped me from touching it. The rest however, was overrun with fear at what that type of power in the wrong hands – the hands of the Gemini Clan, could do.

Slowly, I watched as Finn began to creep closer, as though he was an animal stalking its prey – waiting for the right time to strike. Bracing myself for his next move, I eyed him cautiously, noting the entranced state he seemed to be in.

It was like something had taken complete control of his mind. Whether it was pure awe at the weapon before him or a side effect of slumming with cold-hearted killers over the past week, I couldn't be sure.

Pulling the stun gun from my belt, I gripped it tightly between my hands.

Finn's gaze shifted towards me, clicking his tongue. "You want to play the hero?" he asked, making the task at hand all the more daunting. "That could very easily get you killed."

"It's better than letting that dagger fall into the wrong hands."

With the barrel of the gun aimed at his chest, giving me the best possible chance, I kept my eyes locked on his. He took one step closer, and then another. With each movement, I told myself to pull the trigger, to end this, but every time I felt myself falter.

Then, suddenly, he was right in front of me. The gun was mere inches from his chest, and yet still, I hesitated.

"You may have the will to shoot me, Aspen, but you don't have the strength," he taunted, a knowing smirk hovering on his lips. "Am I right?"

"No – "

A scream cut off my words – my own, I realized, as I watched Finn crumple to the ground. I stumbled backwards until I hit the stone wall behind me, the gun still in my grip as my hands fell to my sides. But I hadn't squeezed the trigger. Whatever was happening, it wasn't because of me.

He wrestled against what appeared to be a ghost as he brought his hands up to his neck, gripping onto the air and struggled to move. It took a few seconds, but with a grunt and a push of momentum he managed to break free, immediately turning to face the invisible force that was fighting against him.

And then it clicked.

The invisibility cloak.

Finn fought blindly, his punches and kicks thrown wide, attempting to restrict her movements and keep her from skirting around him. When she made a move against him however – a carefully planned punch straight to the jaw, he barely acknowledged it. Instead, he immediately reached out to grab her, and in one swift movement had spun her around, trapped her against his chest with his arms around her neck, and yanked the invisibility cloak to the ground.

"You've been out of the field too long," he said, his grip on Kira becoming tighter. "You've lost your touch."

"Funny," Kira said, her voice a rough wheeze, "because I thought, for a second there, I caught you off guard."

"And now you're going to regret it."

I scrambled to reposition the gun in my hands as Finn reached into a small pocket in his belt and pulled out a small syringe. I couldn't shoot, knowing I'd hurt Kira in the process, so I dropped the gun. Rushing across the few meters that separated us, I skidded to a stop as I watched Finn plunge the needle into the side of her neck and released the hold he had on her.

The effects were instant as she collapsed to the floor unconscious, her eyes falling shut as she went.

I ground my teeth together as Finn turned to face me. "What. Did. You. Do?"

"Nothing that'll harm her long term," he replied, a twisted grin forming on his lips. "At least not yet."

Having dropped the now-empty syringe, he lifted his hand so that I could catch a glimpse at what was now in his possession. My eyes widened at the small device.

A bomb.

"All I have to do is activate it," Finn drawled. "Then there'll be only a few minutes before this place comes crumbling down, stone by stone. And by that time, me, and the dagger, will be long gone."

He thought it was that easy? That he'd just deal with me, make a grab for the dagger, and hightail it out of here without a scratch?

I didn't think so.

A switch flicked inside me as I pushed hard against his chest, causing him to waver only slightly in his stance. It was enough however, for me to catch him off guard as I ducked to the ground, swinging my leg around in a powerful kick that swept his legs out from underneath him.

With Finn on his back, I spun on my heel and dove for where I'd let the stun gun clatter to the ground, but this time I didn't hesitate. When it was once again within my grip, I turned my body so that I had a clear shot and pressed the trigger.

The blue-tinged blast that erupted out of the barrel was small, but powerful. He was down – completely immobilized. I breathed a quick sigh of relief as I scrambled up to my feet, but as a rhythmic ticking hit my ears, my blood ran cold.

The bomb was still nestled within the slackened grip of his left hand, but the timer had been set off, each tick signaling one less second I had to get out.

If I moved quickly, it was possible that I could make it up the stairs before it went off, but that still didn't guarantee me safety. This whole building was made of stone – or at least it appeared to be. If the explosion was strong enough to demolish the supports down here, then who knows what kind of damage would be done to the rest of the building.

But I couldn't think like that. I had to believe that I'd make it out of here. That everything would be okay.

The only problem I faced? Figuring out what to do next.

It was a quick decision to leave the dagger behind. I couldn't risk accidentally touching the blade, and perhaps if it was trapped beneath piles of stone, it'd be safer. After all, a lost weapon was harder to locate than a hidden one.

The tough part to swallow was knowing that I didn't have the strength to carry both Finn and Kira to safety. Even after everything he'd done, I knew Finn didn't deserve to be left behind, but if I couldn't save them both, I would do everything I could to save the one who'd had my back since this whole adventure began.

Moving to Kira's side, I brought my arms around her chest, lifting her so that she sat upright. Before she could slump back down to the floor, I threw one of her arms over my shoulders, holding it steady while I wrapped my other arm around her back and stood up, bringing her with me.

Supporting Kira's body with my own, I didn't glance back at Finn as I made my way to the exit, but I figured there was no more than a minute – two max – until the bomb went off.

Not enough time to escape, but long enough to get the two of us as far away from the explosion as possible.

The staircase was just wide enough for me to maneuver both of our bodies up the still slippery steps, and though every movement I made signaled a new pain in my muscles, I kept moving.

I couldn't give up.

Pushing forward, I felt my heart begin to race with adrenaline as I struggled to fight off the burning in my legs and the tremors in my arms. Each small step felt like a mile-high mountain, an impossible challenge that I was somehow mastering, and when the top of the staircase finally came into view I almost wept.

But then the stones began to rumble.

There was no time to process what was happening as the bomb went off. Walls around us began to cave in on themselves and I was thrown off balance, tilting sideways before I fell to the ground.

Pain rushed through me and the last bit of hope I had shattered, but through it all I didn't let go of Kira. Not when I felt the sharp scrape of a stone fall across the side of my face, not when the scream of piercing pain escaped my lungs, and not moments later, when I felt myself succumb to the horrors around me and let it all fade slowly away.

Epilogue

Though I was surrounded by a thick, grey haze, I was still able to make out the scenes that flashed before me. Crumbling buildings, bright flares, smears of blood, and dominating flames – all accompanied by the repetitive sounds of gun shots in the distance and the thundering blast of a bomb.

Everything wove seamlessly together in my mind, casting me as a helpless onlooker with no power to keep the events from unraveling.

It was like I was stuck in a dream – a nightmare – and unable to wake up.

But just like when I'd first arrived, when I finally found the strength to open my eyes, I was faced with the reality that it had not been a dream.

A dull pounding began behind my temples as I blinked, my surroundings fading into view. I was in the Grand Hall, but things were different than before. Instead of a space where agents were free to enjoy their down time with a meal and good company, it'd been completely transformed to resemble a large infirmary. Tables that had previously been used to eat at were now being used as makeshift beds for the injured, with blankets thrown across them to give a semblance of comfort. One food counter remained open, serving those who had the strength to move about, but otherwise, the ambience flooding the Grand Hall was a somber one.

It was a scene that made me wince, wondering what state the rest of the building was in. Because if memory served me right, we'd been somewhere well below the east wing – underneath the library, infirmary, labs, and study rooms – when the bomb had gone off.

And suddenly everything came rushing back to me, my headache growing larger as I made a move to sit up. I remembered the way the ground shook and the fear that shot through me as the stones began to fall, closing me in. But what worried me the most were the unknowns – the events I'd missed while I'd been out.

What had happened to the dagger? To the Gemini Clan? To my friends and the other S.I.C.O agents?

My heart was speeding up with worry when a nurse came rushing over, noticing that I was awake. "Here," she said, picking up a small amount of healing solution and a glass of water from a cart a few feet away. Handing them to me, she smiled encouragingly. "Drink these. They'll make you feel better."

With shaky hands, I reached for them, lifting the water to my lips first. "Thanks," I replied, the cold water soothing my parched throat. As I then took the healing solution, cringing at the unpleasant taste it left in my mouth, the nurse used the opportunity to look over me.

Still adorning the same clothes I'd worn in the fight, I knew that I looked a mess. There were tears in my pants and my shirt, revealing the bruising skin beneath, and in the aftermath of the events, I was covered in a mixture of dust, dirt, and – though I didn't want to think much about it – I was positive the dried patches of crimson alluded to blood lost. If it all belonged to me, I wasn't sure.

My appearance however, was the least of my worries. Besides the pounding inside my head, the muscles in my arm and legs were starting to cramp, having been completely worn out, and with each small move I made, my back screamed in agony. My entire body was protesting, and while I knew that the healing solution would eventually work its magic, I expected to have to suffer through the pain for at least another couple of hours.

When the nurse's eyes finally came back to meet my own, I did my best to conceal my misery. "Do you need anything else?"

Her tone suggested that she believed I was more hurt than I was letting on, but I held my tongue, shaking my head in response. She hovered at my side for a moment longer, but when I said nothing more, she turned to walk away, moving to check on other agents.

Letting out a slow breath, my shoulders sagged and I closed my eyes, wanting just one minute to try and replay everything I'd done, wondering if there'd been another option. A safer option. But there was no time, because as the groaning of wood beside me caught my attention, I turned my head to see that Catherine was occupying the makeshift bed beside mine.

"Aspen," she said, her voice hoarse. Joe was by her side and I watched as he leaned closer to her, muttering something in her ear before she shook her head. "You're alright."

My eyes widened as I took her in. Her skin had lost a significant amount of colour, now a sickly pale shade, only made worse with the darkening shadows underneath her eyes. She lay down, seemingly too weak to move with an IV hooked up to her left arm and a large bandage wrapped around her abdomen.

"Wh-what happened?" I stuttered, flicking my gaze back and forth between them. "Are you alright?"

"I'm fine," she insisted, though the strain in her words had me full of disbelief.

"What she means," Joe cut in before I could push, "is that she will be fine." He glanced at Catherine, meeting her gaze and having a silent conversation for a moment before turning back to me. "Damon cornered her in the attack."

My breath caught, remembering what Finn had said about Damon wanting to take care of Catherine. While he'd used the information to taunt me, he'd also been telling the truth.

"Now your mother here is strong, and has the capability to take on whoever stands in her way of getting things done, but when someone brings a gun into the mix, the stakes always get higher."

It was the first time that I wasn't objecting to someone referring to Catherine as my mom – partially due to the lightning bolt of worry that coursed through me at the word gun. "You were shot?"

"It'll heal," Catherine replied. "Before long it'll be nothing more than a scratch."

I was glad someone seemed to be looking on the bright side, because in that moment, I sure wasn't. "And Damon?" I asked, fearing for what I'd hear in response. "What happened to him?"

"When the bomb went off, like so many of the other Gemini agents, he tried to flee," Joe started to explain, leaving me waiting in anticipation as he paused. "But he didn't get far." I uttered a curse of relief under my breath. "As soon as the alarms went off we were able to contact S.I.C.O headquarters, and as we held off the Gemini Clan, they worked quickly to get here. Damon was caught and detained, as were many of the others."

"So, he'll be locked up?"

"First he'll be questioned, and likely administered a truth serum if he doesn't talk," Joe replied, "but yes. After S.I.C.O gets the information they need, he'll be confined to one of the prison cells they have scattered across the globe."

It was good news. Finally, after weeks of not knowing what would come of the Gemini Clan's advances, I should've been able to breathe easier now that things had ended in our favour. In theory. Instead, I could feel the pressure of unanswered questions – the unknowns – pressing in on me from every direction.

The only way to relieve it? Answers.

"And Finn?" I asked, a tremble to my voice. Though some part of my subconscious already knew the answer I'd get.

I saw the wave of sadness that smoothed over Catherine's features, and let out a breathy sigh as she managed to gently move her head back and forth. Despite his actions, I couldn't stop the ache that spread in my chest as I listened to Joe say the words. That he'd died in the explosion.

"He made his choices, Aspen," Catherine spoke quietly, and I managed to just keep the tears that glazed my eyes at bay, "and there's nothing you could've done to save him."

"But if I'd said something earlier – about suspecting that he was the one working against us, he could still be alive."

"There's no use stressing the past. What you did was brave, albeit rash and dangerous," Joe paused, looking at me pointedly. I shrank back, a small, guilty smile pulling at my lips. "But because of it, Finn never got a hold of the dagger. When everything was dug up, we were able to get you and Kira out, as well as Finn's body, and the dagger was secured. It's in the possession of S.I.C.O headquarters now, and they'll decide what comes of it."

"Kira," I said immediately, "oh my god, is she alright? And what about Beckett, and everyone else?"

"Beckett's been spending time talking things through with the agents that came from headquarters. There were barely a few scrapes on him when all was said and done, but Kira," Joe's voice dropped as he trailed off. "She's been treated and the nurses believe she'll make a full recovery, but the damage was bad. As far as I know, she hasn't woken up yet."

I gulped, but it'd do me no good to worry. I had to trust that the nurses knew what they were doing; had to believe that Kira would be okay.

"So, what do we do now?" I asked, my gaze darting between Catherine and Joe. "With everything that's happened, is it safe to stay here, or...?"

A look of uncertainty filled Catherine's eyes, and I noticed the way that Joe reached for one of her hands as she mustered the breath to speak. "For now, given the damages that have been done, Division 27 is being disbanded. S.I.C.O is working hard to send every agent to the Division that they believe will be the best fit, but I've been asked to help out at headquarters for a while, as has Joe. And you, Aspen, have a choice."

My brows furrowed in confusion.

"I never wanted this life for you," she admitted. "The danger, the constant worrying, and the large question marks that come with each assignment. And now that the Gemini Clan no longer poses an imminent threat, if you choose, you can leave S.I.C.O behind and go back to the life you knew. It may not be completely safe going back home, but if you want a normal life, you're free to go anywhere and have it." She paused for a moment as I took in that information. "Or... you can choose to stay. I wanted to ask if you'd consider coming with us. I'd like the chance to get to know the daughter I gave up, and the woman you've grown up to be, but only if it's what you want as well."

She was giving me a choice, unlike when I'd first arrived. If it'd been two months prior, there wouldn't have been any hesitation on my end as I took the opportunity to leave this all behind. But now, after gaining friends whom I could trust to have my back and beginning the journey of becoming a S.I.C.O agent, my perspective had changed.

I wasn't the same girl who'd been brought here against her will. I was stronger, and in that moment, I realized that I didn't want to go back. I'd come so far, and I wasn't ready for everything to unravel.

"Yeah," I said, a genuine smile pulling at my lips as I met Catherine's gaze, "I think I'd like that."

It was a few hours later when I began to feel the effects of the healing solution. The pain was still there, but it was dimming, and even though they advised against moving around too much, I managed to convince one of the nurses to take me to see Kira.

She had been set up atop one of the tables on the other side of the Grand Hall, and though I did believe the nurses were telling the truth, that she'd be okay, I needed to see it for myself.

As I slowly limped my way through the hordes of people, a nurse at my side for support, I saw for the first time all the damage that'd been done. It seemed like almost everyone had obtained some kind of injury in the fight – some much more severe than others. There were stitched up cuts and broken bones. Bruised skin and exhausted eyes. And then there were the heartbroken ones, those who'd lost a friend and were mourning the agents that hadn't made it out of the fight alive.

By the time I reached Kira's side, the nausea in my stomach had grown to insurmountable heights, and I was forced to take long, deep breaths to dispel just a fraction of the worrying thoughts that were consuming me. Sitting down on the bench of the table, I thanked the nurse for her help, though it came out as more of a wheeze, and she nodded in acknowledgement before leaving me alone.

Shifting my gaze over to Kira, I felt my chin begin to tremble. She was certainly worse off than I was, and it was all because of that serum Finn had used on her. I'd asked the nurse what it'd been, and was shocked to learn that it hadn't been the same thing that Beckett had used on me the first night we'd met. It was more destructive. It hadn't just left her unconscious, but had weakened her from the inside, making the physical blows from the explosion all the more impactful.

Her eyes were still closed, but her breathing was steady as I took one of her hands and squeezed it between my own. "Please," I said softly, willing her to awaken, "please be okay."

As the minutes passed, there wasn't so much as a twitch from her body. Periodically, a nurse would come around to offer me something to eat, but eating was the last thing on my mind. In fact, even the thought of forcing food into my body, no matter how rational it was, made my stomach twist.

Instead, I sat there, waiting for hours until her hand finally moved in mine, squeezing it as she was pulled into consciousness.

"Kira," I breathed out with relief as her eyes fluttered open.

Her features scrunched up in pain as she moved slightly, rustling the blankets she lay on. "I'm guessing this means everything worked out?" she asked, her voice scratchy.

My laughter was woven with choked back tears and pure joy. "Yeah, for the most part," I replied, watching as her dried lips stretched into a thin smile. "Kira, I have to ask... how did you even know where I was? What I was planning to do?"

"I didn't," she replied, "but I was tasked with watching the security cameras and helping stand guard of the labs. If I hadn't seen you disappear after that cloud of smoke you released, I wouldn't have realized what you were doing."

Suddenly, I found myself overcome by a pang of guilt. "But you didn't have to follow – "

She was quick to cut me off. "I know I didn't have to, but that's what friends are for. Though I didn't know that Finn had followed you until I saw all the guards that'd been stationed outside the tunnel completely down for the count." For a moment, a horror spread through me, knowing that when Finn had come after me, he clearly hadn't spared any-one. "And at that point, there was no time to grab any back up. I knew I had to get to you."

"Honestly, if you hadn't come when you did, I don't know what I would've done," I admitted, knowing that I'd been overrun with nerves and had been seconds away from back-ing down. "But I'm so sorry that I got you into that mess. If I hadn't – "

"Don't apologize," she said, cutting me off once more. "Every agent knows that even if it's dangerous, sometimes following your instincts is the best way to get things done.

Plus, if I had to choose again, I wouldn't do anything differently."

There was a moment where an unrecognizable emotion crossed her features, almost like a mixture of grief and understanding, but before I could ask her what was wrong, she spoke again.

"There's something..." she paused, as though struggling to hold back tears. "I've never told you the real reason behind my transfer into the lab."

From the tenderness of her words, I didn't know if I was ready to hear the story, but nevertheless, I held onto her hand as she told it.

"Her name was Raven," she said eventually, exhaling slowly. "She was gorgeous, strong, and fearless. I spent a lot of my childhood wondering if something was wrong with me, wondering why I'd been born attracted to girls instead of guys, but after meeting her, everything kind of fell into place." There was a whisper of a smile on her lips, because even though her memories were painful, she cherished them.

"We were together through it all – training, our first assignments – and when we were paired up for an assignment after so long, there was a comfort knowing that I'd be there to keep her safe, instead of waiting up for her to come back to me. But things went to shit that night. I accidentally set off a hidden alarm while doing surveillance and the next thing I knew, the sound of gun shots ripped through the night. And if... if she hadn't jumped in front of me... if she hadn't taken the bullet for me... she'd still be here." The tears were falling by this point, and each word was a hiccup that she had to force out. "She sacrificed herself for me, and after that... after that I never went out into the field again. Not until I ran after you, because in some part of my brain, I thought that protecting a friend – putting my life on the line – would prove to the gods above that I was worthy of being hers, even if it was just for a short moment in time."

The story absolutely broke my heart, even more so as it ended and I watched her completely fall apart. I'd have never guessed that Kira, someone who appeared to be the epitome of confidence and strength, had carried the weight of her girlfriend's death on her shoulders. And after so long, there'd been nothing pushing her to face her past. She could've stayed in the lab and alerted someone else of my whereabouts, but she hadn't. She stepped out and fought for me – like a true friend – and a lumped formed in my throat knowing what it cost her emotionally to do so.

"There's not a doubt in my mind that she's watching over you right now and smiling, because there's no way she's anything but proud of you," I said softly, smiling through the tears. "And so am I."

She squeezed my hand, but even I could see that through the emotional turmoil she'd just put herself through, her energy was dwindling.

"Get some rest," I said, and her eyes were already closing as I added, "and when you wake up, you can tell me all about Raven, and every way that she stole your heart."

I called over the closest nurse as Kira's breathing evened out. As I watched her get checked over, the worries in my mind slowly began to vanish, because I knew that I didn't need to hope anymore – I knew she'd be okay.

When I awoke the next morning, I was in my room, the sun hitting my face as it shone brightly through the cracked glass of the window.

Instead of bringing me back to the place I'd taken up beside Catherine, the nurses had deemed me well enough to head back to the housing wing for the night – which had attained the least amount of damage. And now, as I slid out from underneath the covers and trotted across the room to my en-suite, I reveled in the way the healing solution had worked its way through my body. The aches and pains that'd been front and center the day previous were now gone, leaving only the physical scars to remain.

After a lengthened shower, in which I stood under the spray until every last piece of evidence from the fight had been washed away, I let my damp hair fall down over my shoulders and pulled on a fresh set of clothes.

It was a new day and I was feeling better. Not quite 100% yet, but good enough that I wanted to venture out onto the grounds, needing to see for myself the damage that'd been done.

Making my way down the stairs, I saw the cracks that now adorned the stone I walked on, and as I reached the bottom, noticed the security tape that had been hung up to keep everyone from exploring the east wing. From here I could see large pieces of stone littering the hall, and could only imagine the extent of the damage beyond.

Stepping outside, I could hear the faint chirps of birds in the distance as they flew over head. A mild breeze kissed my skin and there wasn't a cloud in the sky, making it seem like a perfect spring day – if it weren't for the state of the Division.

Careful of scattered debris, I made my way slowly around the grounds with no real destination in mind.

Over a quarter of the building was left in ruins. As expected, the most damage had been in the east wing, and as I got a better look, I saw nothing but complete demolition. There was nothing left but a pile of stones, though beneath them, it was likely that items such as clocks, chairs, books, and so many other miscellaneous things, remained within the rubble.

Around where the east wing had previously stood, that which remained was considerably worse for wear. Charred stone, shattered windows, and smaller piles of fallen stone made up the remainder of the scene, forming such a contrast to the view I'd grown used to.

As I rounded the edge of the building, a wisp of happiness flowed through me as I saw that the gazebo remained relatively intact.

Walking up the cracked steps, I pulled open the flimsy door and moved towards the center of the enclosed space. From where I stood, I could see both the horrors that the Gemini Clan and Finn had thrust upon the Division, as well as the horizon that reached well beyond the forest. There'd be no way to forget the events; the knowledge that there'd been blood spilt on these very grounds, and the memories would always linger in the back of my mind, but in that moment,

I chose to look towards the horizon – towards what would surely be a new beginning.

I must've lost track of time, because before I knew it, the sound of footsteps hit my ears and the door squeaked open.

"Hey."

A soft smile pulled at my lips as I turned to face Beckett. "Hey," I returned, my eyes scanning over him as he continued towards me, coming to a stop just inches away from me. "How are you?"

"I'm good. Just a few scratches," he said, lifting a hand to the side of my face before running the back of his fingers softly over my cuts. "It's nothing I can't handle."

I wanted to bring up what had happened – the way I'd kissed him out of the blue, only to disappear and put my life on the line, but he didn't give me the chance. Before I could find the words, he brought his lips down onto my own. Applying a light pressure at first, I felt a thrill of euphoria stream through me, and once the surprise wore off, I didn't hesitate to kiss him back. Our lips moved in unison, equally as demanding, and when I felt the sweep of his tongue across my bottom lip, a shiver raced down my spine as I opened my mouth wider to give him better access.

From there, everything escalated. The pace picked up, and while my hands had previously been clutching the front of his shirt, they slowly inched upwards, exploring the panes of his chest, the muscles in his arms, and the strength in his shoulders as they went. I could feel him smile against my lips as I pushed myself closer to him, craving the safety that he offered, and just as a quiet moan escaped my lips, he began to lighten his movements.

"You scared me half to death," Beckett said as he pulled away, my eyes still closed as his breath fanned my lips. When I slowly forced them open, I saw the complex emotion that stared back at me. "What were you thinking going down that tunnel?"

"I don't know if I was, to be honest," I replied, moving my hands to hold either side of his face. "I just knew that there were so many people fighting to keep the Gemini Clan at bay, including yourself, and I wanted to help. I had figured out where the dagger was hidden, and I don't know, some part of me just knew that it wasn't as protected as it should've been."

His arms dropped to hang loosely around my waist. "I'm not saying I'm not proud of you, because I am," he said, an underlying softness to his words, "but when the bomb went off and no one could find you, I felt the ground beneath me shift. And when you were dragged from underneath all that stone, Aspen, I don't know if I can ever forget the burst of relief I felt when they said you were going to be okay."

I lifted upwards, landing a quick peck on his lips. "I'm a fighter, you know that firsthand," I replied, trying to make light of the situation. There was nothing to worry about now. The worst of it was behind us. "I guess you'll just have to get used to the fact that you're not the only one willing to risk their lives for the greater good."

A wariness filled his features. "Yeah, about that," he started. "For the past few weeks, my assignments have been geared more towards surveillance work for agents at the S.I.C.O headquarters. They're looking to reclaim the other two remaining weapons from the Gemini Clan, and now that the dagger is in their hands, well, they're moving forward with their efforts. I'll be heading there once everything here is sorted."

From the way he was looking at me, anticipating my response, I knew he expected a different reaction than the one I gave. "Well it just so happens, that my mom is also being transferred to headquarters for a while." I smiled up at him. "And when she asked, I told her I'd go with her."

His expression was one of surprise and happiness. "Seriously?"

I nodded. "It may not have been what I saw myself doing with my life, but being a part of S.I.C.O, being an agent, it's what I want now. I want to continue training, I want to prove to myself that I have what it takes, and maybe, just maybe, I want to get skilled enough to take you down in a fight."

Laughter escaped his lips. "You can try," he teased, before planting his lips on mine once more. It was a soft kiss, but one filled with passion and yearning all the same.

When he pulled back a minute later, Beckett slipped his arms around my shoulders, tucking me in close to him. I felt his cheek rest softly against the top of my head and I sighed in contentment as I wrapped an arm around his waist.

I didn't know what was ahead for me, for us, but I couldn't wait to find out.